Canals are my home

Dedication

I would like to dedicate this book to Frank Challis
— Thames bargebuilder from 1905-1961. He
worked for the firm of William Cory Ltd at
Charlton for more than thirty years and was always
known to his workmates and friends up and down
the river as Dolly — a name given to him when he
was sent to work as an apprentice at the age of
fourteen, dressed in a black velevet suit with white
lace cuffs ... but he was always known to me as ...
MY DAD.

Canals are my home

Iris Bryce

 Kenneth Mason

British Library Cataloguing in Publication Data
Bryce, Iris
    Canals are my home.
    1.   Canals - England
    I.   Title
    386'.46'0924   HE436

    ISBN 0-85937-171-9

Published by Kenneth Mason, Homewell, Havant, Hampshire

Printed in Great Britain by Coasbyprint Limited, Claybank Road, Portsmouth, Hampshire

Contents

Illustrations

Acknowledgement is made to British Waterways Board for use of pictures 7, 9, 10, 11, 12, 16; Birmingham Post 1 and Derek Pratt 4.

1

'There she is – all five ton of her,' and he pointed through the doorway of the steelworks towards a long, long, very narrow metal shell.

If he'd said 50 tons, I would have believed him. I looked again at what was to be my new home. Of course, the whole thing was absurd; no one could ever actually live in such a confined space. All right for holidays but not as a home for … weeks … months … years …

'Don't look so worried,' – it was Peter Ellis, the boatbuilder, again. 'In another three weeks or so you won't recognise it; just wait until John and Pete start fitting her out.'

And he was right. By the time we had made two or three more visits to discuss size of wardrobe, storage space for bed linen, chosen carpets, blinds and found to my great pleasure that my Ercol dining table and the bottom half of the sideboard to match it would pass through the doorway, the excitement flooded back … the excitement that had started only nine months before.

We'd been sitting at breakfast in our Kentish farmhouse, discussing the startling news received in the morning mail. By a series of what had first been quite unrelated incidents, we had come to realise the value of our property – and here it was this morning, in writing. £45,000! We didn't speak at first as the letter was passed across the table, we were too stunned, but my thoughts were whirring.

The four children were grown up and had left home. Three were married, so we were living in a house with far too many rooms, still working seven days a week on our small-holding which, apart from providing us with all the food and fuel we needed, did little else. Owen voiced my thoughts, 'seems stupid to keep on working, at least here, doesn't it?'

That started the discussion: if we sold the farmhouse where would we go? All property was fairly expensive in our area, so what could we do with ourselves? Apart from farming, we could both write articles, and lecture. Owen was also a jazz musician who taught and played regularly all over the country. Now that was an idea: suppose we travelled England, playing and lecturing now and again, exploring towns, villages and cities. Who knew, we might even find somewhere nicer than Kent to settle down in finally. 'Why don't we build a narrow boat and live on the canals – you've always said it's the best way to see England,' the words seemed to surprise Owen as much as they did me.

Keen boaters that we were, we had had only a week at a time on a boat for holidays, but … why not?

Out came the only boating magazine, *Waterways World*, then catering for our kind of water travel. We took it monthly and had quite a collection of back numbers. We read through the advertisements and finally chose four companies to write to, two large and two small. We sent a simple design asking them to quote for a boat which provided all-the-year-round living accommodation and, whatever else, had to include a music room large enough to take an upright piano!

We wrote a second letter at the same time ... to the estate agents putting up the farm for sale.

How easy it all was. We were soon visiting each of the boatyards in turn to discuss the why and why nots, to look at the workmanship offered and, what was to us very important, delivery dates. We chose one of the smaller firms, Fernie Steel, to build our boat, and their sister company, Blisworth Tunnel Boats to fit it out. Work, we were told, would start at the end of May.

The summer was always a busy time for us on the farm but the weeks just flew by in 1974, for not only were we still growing a few crops in the vegetable field, but we had also to keep interrupting our work to show prospective buyers over the house, garden and farm. I was astonished to receive a 'phone call from Peter Ellis one evening, asking if we could get the piano to the steel works in Market Harborough, as they had reached the stage where if the piano didn't go in now, it never would. It had to be put on board before the final piece of roof was welded on as the doorways were too small!

All the boatyards had shown interest in our design when they saw the music room, plus piano, but we had not expected the celebrity treatment we received when we delivered it. The piano had belonged to my parents who had bought it in 1923 since when it had had plenty of use in its 50 years of life. It was far from beautiful to look at but the tone was good. As we drove into the yard of the steelworks, we were met by Peter who nodded towards the outside staircase leading to his office and said, 'you'd better go up and make yourselves known to the press. They've been drinking my coffee and worrying my secretary for two hours now.' Puzzled, we did as we were told and upon entering the tiny office, perched high above the floor of the steelyard, we were immediately bombarded with questions, while cameras clicked and lights flashed. Then we were pushed downstairs again to pose alongside the fork-lift truck that was now precariously swinging our piano into the air and down into the steel shell of our narrow boat. All very exciting, but not half as exciting apparently as the following day when we were back home in Kent. A television camera crew arrived 24 hours late to film the piano going on board. On being told by Peter Ellis that they were a day adrift, they calmly said that as a 'slot' had been left for this unusual news item, it just had to be filled. There was only one thing to do — and they did it. The fork-lift truck was hired again and this time it took the piano off the boat and then put it back on again for the benefit of the TV cameras.

Back home, I now started to think about how I would carry out daily household chores in a space only 6 feet 10 inches wide. I got out the plan of my new home – 65 feet long, divided up into music room eight feet long, bedroom eight feet, lavatory/shower three feet, galley seven feet, open plan lounge 30 feet, the rest of the boat's length being taken up front and stern.

All the floors were carpeted with the exception of the galley which was covered in a vinyl type lino with a washable pile rug on top. I had bought a small carpet sweeper which looked like a child's toy to me, but it worked adequately and was just the right height when it came to storing it in the lavatory compartment. It rested nicely between the Elsan and the side of the boat with its handle tucked underneath the window ledge.

Cooking would be on a full size gas cooker alongside which a gas fridge fitted neatly with a working surface on top.

I decided that I'd have to use launderettes for my washing, at least the larger items. I could easily do the smalls in my large stainless steel sink, but how would I dry them? I decided to write for advice to a leading women's magazine, and asked at the same time about irons suitable to run off 12 volts.

They replied promptly and pleasantly about my embarking on such an adventurous way of life. They went on to say how everyone in the office envied me the peaceful get-away-from-it-all existence and they finished up by enclosing details of electric drying cupboards, airers and spin dryers – all using 240 volts!

So I rang an electric iron manufacturer with my problems and after repeating my query to several departments, eventually found myself talking to the managing director. He knew my plight exactly – his wife was faced with the same situation every year when they took their yacht to sea for their annual four months cruise! 'Only one thing you can do,' he advised. 'Cut the flex off and use your electric iron on the gas stove, as we do.'

I thought this rather drastic. Surely, I pleaded with him, there must be some irons made not using 240 volts.

'Ah now, if you were in prison I could help you. We make a special 50 volt one for them.' A hearty laugh followed. 'No, you'll just have to say goodbye to your flex.'

However, I decided to look at the Calor gas irons available before operating on my electric one but the only one I could find was cumbersome to use and would take a lot of storage space. So my poor electric iron suffered an amputation.

Long before we finally moved on to the boat, the farm kitchen was looking bare. My three married daughters lived near enough to visit us fairly frequently, especially during warm summer days when our swimming pool tempted them as much as our strawberries. Now, however, they found time to stand in the kitchen and make remarks like, 'you won't be able to use your food mixer on the boat will you? ... or coffee grinder ... liquidiser ... even the fridge.' Linda's present one was a hand-me-down third time and always on the blink. My electric hostess trolley followed the fridge, but in the direction of Tunbridge Wells and Marny's house.

Back at the boatyard, things went so smoothly that we no longer visited Market Harborough. Our boat was now being fitted out by the boat-

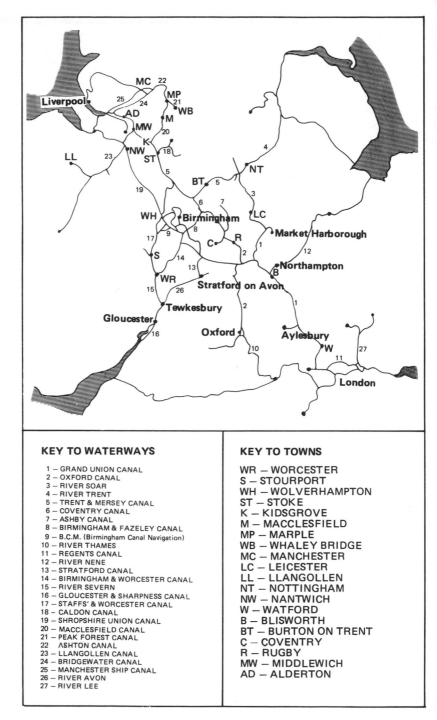

KEY TO WATERWAYS

1 – GRAND UNION CANAL
2 – OXFORD CANAL
3 – RIVER SOAR
4 – RIVER TRENT
5 – TRENT & MERSEY CANAL
6 – COVENTRY CANAL
7 – ASHBY CANAL
8 – BIRMINGHAM & FAZELEY CANAL
9 – B.C.M. (Birmingham Canal Navigation)
10 – RIVER THAMES
11 – REGENTS CANAL
12 – RIVER NENE
13 – STRATFORD CANAL
14 – BIRMINGHAM & WORCESTER CANAL
15 – RIVER SEVERN
16 – GLOUCESTER & SHARPNESS CANAL
17 – STAFFS' & WORCESTER CANAL
18 – CALDON CANAL
19 – SHROPSHIRE UNION CANAL
20 – MACCLESFIELD CANAL
21 – PEAK FOREST CANAL
22 – ASHTON CANAL
23 – LLANGOLLEN CANAL
24 – BRIDGEWATER CANAL
25 – MANCHESTER SHIP CANAL
26 – RIVER AVON
27 – RIVER LEE

KEY TO TOWNS

WR – WORCESTER
S – STOURPORT
WH – WOLVERHAMPTON
ST – STOKE
K – KIDSGROVE
M – MACCLESFIELD
MP – MARPLE
WB – WHALEY BRIDGE
MC – MANCHESTER
LC – LEICESTER
LL – LLANGOLLEN
NT – NOTTINGHAM
NW – NANTWICH
W – WATFORD
B – BLISWORTH
BT – BURTON ON TRENT
C – COVENTRY
R – RUGBY
MW – MIDDLEWICH
AD – ALDERTON

builder's father at Blisworth, on the Grand Union Canal, near Northampton. By the end of August, all we had to decide was the style of lettering for the boat's name. The name itself had been no problem: it was to be *Bix* in honour of the great jazz trumpeter Bix Beiderbecke. We decided on simple black letters against a white background. These stood out well against the rest of the boat which had white sides and blue roof with a black hull.

In September, she was fully complete ... all carpets laid, window blinds fitted, gas, water, heaters, Elsan, the galley complete with pots, pans, china, cutlery, the bed linen stored beneath our four foot by six foot bed and even three of my pictures hanging up in the lounge. All it now needed was us on board before the SR3 Lister diesel engine sprung into action and carried us away ... but we still had the farm. Dozens of people had looked at it but no one wanted it.

The agents suggested an auction and we readily agreed, a date being fixed for October.

We were now spending three days a week on the boat, taking short trips along the Grand Union, usually to Weedon and back, while for the rest of the week we wandered around a now empty farm, trying to make it look as tidy as possible, difficult when there are no chickens in the yards, no winter crops in the fields and the weeds and undergrowth start to take over. The farmhouse was almost bare, with no carpets, one bed and a minimum of crockery and cutlery.

Tempers got rather short as the lure of the boat became stronger. I almost came to hating my home. At last the auction notices went up and within two days many thousands of other notices went up all over the country for another event taking place on the same day — a general election!

Twenty-eight people turned up at the auction rooms. Two properties were for sale: our farm and a beautiful Kentish yeoman's cottage. It was all over in 20 minutes. No one had bid a penny for either of the properties. Our agents suggested that the election was the reason and we'd probably get a 'phone call from a buyer in the morning. We didn't.

Owen and I realised we couldn't continue our lives split between farm and boat and two weeks later we left the farm, told the agents we would ring them once a week and set out for our new home.

2

When we had first told our family and friends that we were selling the farm and moving on to a boat, all asked the same two questions: why? and what about the cats? The second question was invariably followed by a supplementary, 'Can we have them?'

Even a non-cat lover like Owen had to admit that Treacle and Maple were two incredible characters. He was an enormous ginger tom and she a delicate, ethereal princess of cats whose undercoat of silver fur twinkled provocatively through her top glossy black coat. Both cats had been born in the same litter, and never had twins been more unalike.

They were farm cats – in theory. On most cold, wet nights you would find Treacle stretched over half the rug in front of our roaring log fire, whilst Maple always curled up on my lap. During the night, he draped himself over the radiator in the kitchen and she could actually stretch out underneath it.

I had decided that I could not leave the cats behind and that they would share our new life. Our local RSPCA inspector advised against it but I was adamant and he said at last, 'well, keep them shut in the boat for at least a day, then when you first let them out do so before a meal. That should ensure they don't run away, at least the first time. But it won't work, they'll probably run off after a while.'

But I still wanted to have my cats with me, so on a cold Friday morning in November, we arrived at Blisworth by car loaded with the rest of our clothes, books, records, a good supply of food and Treacle and Maple.

We had two problems awaiting us at the boatyard. One was that we couldn't pay for the boat! Until the farm was sold we had no money. Our bank manager had allowed a bridging loan of £2,000 to show Peter that we did have some money. But there was still a balance of £8,000 due. We had arranged to live on board at the yard for a few weeks whilst our finances were sorted out.

The second problem was no permission from the British Waterways Board. We had applied, sent off the money, but still no licence.

We spent that first day putting away books and records and keeping a constant watch on the cats every time the door was opened. I kept looking about me – this was now my home, where I would cook, sleep, eat, and live out my life for the next couple of years. Would I soon miss my large house, my garden, the rose beds, the lawns and swimming pool? What about vegetables and fruit, and just being able to go out and cut or pick whatever I fancied? Then there were the many friends, the social life, the drama group of which I had been a member for 21 years of its 22 years life, its chairman, its secretary, I'd acted, produced, written for it. ...

Such nostalgia was pushed aside the next morning when Peter came on board for coffee and calmly suggested we should start on our two-year exploration of the inland waterways ... and we could pay him when the farm was sold. We were overcome by such a gesture. Here indeed was a fine example of the warmth and friendliness we'd heard so much about when reading or talking of boating people.

As to the licence, Peter had telephoned the British Waterways Board and they too showed munificence. They said we could start cruising immediately and the licence would be sent on as soon as their computer started behaving itself again.

I invited Peter, along with his two young workmen, John and Peter, to have a few drinks with us later that evening. We hadn't had any launching ceremony in view of the unsold farm, but at least we would now have a farewell party.

It was cosy and warm in the boat that night. Treacle and Maple sat close together in front of the gas fire, whilst Owen and I with our three guests sat on the new bed-settee we'd installed for visitors, and our fascinating folding up chair brought back from a holiday in Portugal, which now fitted in so well with our pine interior cabin.

I congratulated John and Pete on their workmanship, 'you've made it so snug and comfortable that I already feel at home, as if it's part of me,' I said. 'Ah,' smiled Pete, 'that's John's carpentry. Always makes it fit nice and snug. Got good training for that didn't you John?'

John nodded. 'Oh yes, everything had to be just right, like you said, snug and comfortable.'

'Was that at another boatyard?' I asked.

'No,' he took a long drink. 'I used to work for an undertaker, made coffins for him.'

Owen almost choked over his glass whilst the three men roared at the sight of my startled face. I took another look around my home – no, it didn't look like a coffin ... yes, it did look like a home.

We'd made no plans, had no routes mapped out. The nose of the boat pointed towards Gayton Junction so that's the way we went. It was a bitterly cold morning, the sky a brittle blue with the sun almost silver, low on the horizon.

Waving goodbye to Blisworth Tunnel Boats, we switched on our engine and floated away up the Grand Union Canal. Half a mile on, at Gayton Junction, we decided to turn off the main canal and go down the Northampton arm. We'd spend a day in Northampton, return down the arm and proceed up the Grand Union, perhaps we'd head for Oxford. Yes, let's go to Oxford. We knew Oxford, had friends at Abingdon ... what a surprise for them.

The Northampton arm is five miles long and falls steeply through 17 locks, 13 of them coming almost on top of one another at Rothersthorpe, which is a small hamlet situated about one mile away from the canal. It is almost opposite Milton Malsor, a slightly larger village. There are no villages actually on the arm and the landscape is just vast tracts of open country, with the M1 noisily hissing its way over the canal itself at the bottom of the Rothersthorpe locks.

We decided to stop for a coffee outside the first lock, to gird our loins as it were, before tackling the work ahead of us. Also, we were both very cold in spite of our new protective nautical clothing. I soon had the gas fire alight and the kettle boiling before I realised that the cats were nowhere to be seen. I called them and started looking under the sideboard, the coffee table; in fact there were so few places that they could have hidden that before Owen had removed his outdoor clothes, I had come to the conclusion that they had got out of the boat somehow and run away. But Owen wouldn't go along with that idea, so we systematically started at the back of the boat in the music room, looking behind the piano, even along the tiny space behind the ladderack fitting, then the bedroom. Here there was only a narrow gap underneath the wardrobe, just enough room to store shoes and slippers. And lying on top of these, squashed almost to pulp was a trembling mass of ginger fur, large green eyes staring out in mute terror.

We extricated Treacle from his hidey-hole and whilst I sat on the settee stroking his quivering coat and talking softly to him, Owen carried on with the hunt for Maple but she seemed to have been spirited away. There was not a sign of her anywhere. I suddenly remembered the guaranteed, never-fail signal that used to bring forth both cats, tearing out of the woods and fields in a frenzied run to the kitchen door. At meal times, all I did was to stand at the door and shake the old glass Horlicks jar containing their cat biscuits. Owen had moved the jar one inch or so when Treacle leapt off my lap, transformed into a prowling tiger once again, and from underneath the sink came the sound of falling tins, jars, boxes, followed by cups and saucers and jugs from the shelves next to the sink, as a pathetic bedraggled Maple appeared. She had found a way into the minute space between the cupboard and the back of the sink unit, entering it from the crockery shelves — and yet in going in she hadn't disturbed one piece of china. She rectified that in her exit of course and I picked up the pieces of two saucers and noticed one cracked cup.

By now, it was too late for morning coffee, but time for early lunch. Over this we came to the conclusion that the cats had been frightened by the actual movement of the boat ... they had heard the engines running while we were in the yard, as we have to run them for at least one hour a day to provide enough electricity for lighting and the water pump. But they had not before felt any movement while the engines roared away; possibly, also, the boat and contents vibrated as we went along. Still, as they now had cleaned up their dishes and were happily at their ablutions, it appeared not to have hurt them too much. In a day or so they would surely have settled down.

We decided to start again, so dressed warmly in over-trousers, anoraks, woolly hats and gloves, we left the warmth inside the boat. Outside the sky had darkened and the wind was whistling down the canal, sending the water along in thousands of tiny white horses. We approached the first lock and I jumped off, windlass in hand. Locks were no mystery to us. With all our boating holidays behind us there wasn't much that we didn't know.

As I pushed, heaved and shoved my seven and a half stone against the balance beam, I realised that this was the first lock I'd operated on my own. During holidays there was always a willing crew of four, five or even six. In fact, I usually only worked locks the first day; the children then took them over as their tasks while I dealt only with the cooking ... the rest of the time I could sit basking in the sunshine in the well deck or on the roof.

Pushing and breathing heavily, I told myself that, like the cats, in a day or two I'd soon find those extra muscles and settle into a routine. Already, my slightly rheumaticky knee twinged less since I'd been jumping on and off the boat.

The lock gate finally moved an inch or so, just as a gust of wind whipped across the open fields. Owen yelled out, 'open the bloody gate – quick.' The nose of the boat swung viciously across the canal as if it was made of tissue paper and not $\frac{1}{4}$-inch steel. Panting and rasping, the wind sucking all the breath out of me, I managed to open the gate and Owen tried to battle with what was now a raging gale and persuade our 6 feet 10 inches boat into the seven foot space of the lock. But each time the wind won and I stood helpless watching in horror as our boat banged and crashed into the stone-sided approach to the lock.

Then the snow started; fine sleet at first, but quickly turning into a blizzard. Somehow or other, Owen headed the boat in the right direction and I clambered aboard to get the front rope. I heard Owen say something about putting it round a bollard, but the wind whipped the rest of the sentence away over the hedges and across the landscape. But I knew what he meant so I did as I was told.

I looped the rope round the bollard but to my horror the ground around it and my feet suddenly rose into the air as the boat continued moving, taking bollard, grass and all with it!!

The next two hours were worse than any nightmare. We stayed in the first lock for half an hour hoping the blizzard would ease. Eventually, the wind dropped sufficiently for us to move out and I ran on ahead to open up the second lock. But the fates were not on our side and once again the boat swung frenziedly to smash against the lock entrance. This time I noticed a long dent appear in our steel side! This lock had almost immovable paddles – used for letting water in and out of the locks – and I was only able to move one ratchet at a time if I took a running jump onto the windlass. This sight sent Owen into hysterics and we both finished up freezing cold, soaking wet and doubled up with laughter.

By the time we had passed through the second lock, the sun was almost setting. It was nearly four o'clock and although it was against all the by-laws of the Waterboard to moor in the pounds between locks, that was the very thing we did. We had to: I was so physically exhausted, that it was impossible to continue.

As we peeled off dripping coats, trousers, gloves, caps and boots, storing them away in the wet cupboard at the back of the music room, I had second thoughts about this wonderful relaxing new life we'd taken on. All I craved now was to soak in a hot, hot bath we no longer possessed. We did have a shower though and, not caring if we used up all the water, we stood together under the blissful hot water together and giggled away at the mess we'd made of our first day.

As I prepared the evening meal, we went over the procedures for mooring and locking. When we tied up, Owen would put the nose of the boat towards the side and I would jump off with the front rope, keeping it fairly slack while he brought in the stern. Before jumping off himself, he would throw the mooring spikes and mallet on to the towpath, then with the stern rope in hand he would leave the boat. Once alongside, the boat remained almost static while we knocked in the spikes and tied up. I could then go on board, light the fires, and start preparing hot drinks or a meal. If it was a permanent night mooring Owen would then go on the roof and erect our television aerial. We had an excellent book supplied by the BBC giving field maps of various television stations and their frequencies and, if near houses, we could see which way their aerials pointed. When it came to locks, it was best, if possible, to leave the boat in time to run ahead and get the gates open, but as the maintenance of most of the locks is far from good, then it was just a case of hoping that I wouldn't have too much of a struggle in carrying this out.

Before sitting down to dinner, I decided it was time the cats left the boat for some exercise. This was very much to Owen's satisfaction as he was more than fed up with continually emptying their dirt box. I had to admit that it wasn't very pleasant having the box in the lounge in full view of the settee, but there really was nowhere else for it.

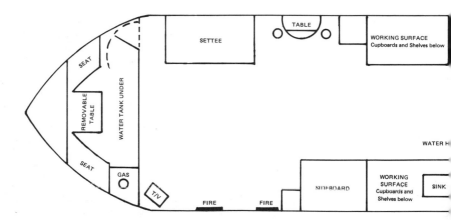

With a cat under each arm, I went to the front of the boat. Owen opened the door and I quickly leaned over and put them on to the towpath. The snow and wind had ceased and the evening was starlit and clear. In the distance we could hear the soft murmur of the traffic hurtling down the M1.

There was a scuffle at my feet and looking down, I saw Treacle and Maple back on deck. I put them back on the towpath again, but as I turned quickly to go inside, they were there before me, almost as if they were on the end of a piece of elastic. We tried again but no sooner had their feet touched the ground than they leapt back on to the boat. But, determined to lose that wretched dirt box, I wrapped up once again and in a still soggy coat, and with wellingtons beneath the long skirt I'd changed into for the evening, I jumped on to the towpath with a cat under each arm. Owen grinned as he shut the door and went back inside the warm boat. I put the cats down on the ground and walked along the crunchy snow and just as they had accompanied me on walks through our own woods, they followed. Only this time, instead of running ahead and chasing exciting smells, they pawed along miserably about two inches from my ankles. I picked them up and put them in the undergrowth, but they just sidled back. I turned suddenly and ran as fast as I could to the boat and banged on the door. As I hurtled through ... they were there before me. Both had used the dirt-box and were washing in front of the gas fire before I'd removed my wellington boots. I was beaten this time and too tired to care. By half past eight we were tucked up for the night, Owen and I under our continental quilt, Treacle under the wardrobe and Maple back under the sink again. But they had better look out tomorrow ... I would get my revenge.

A loud bang woke me up – it was me falling out of the bed! As I tried to

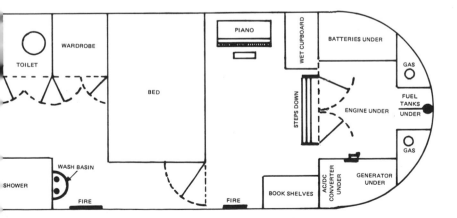

stand up, I wondered if I was really awake; surely I must be in the middle of a fantasy? One in which the whole world is on its side. My view of our bedroom and the remaining 50 feet of boat reminded me of the interior of the Crazy House at the fairground. The whole thing was lop-sided. To walk I almost had one foot on the floor and one on the wall.

Owen looked out of the window and gave a yell. I scrambled up our now sloping bed to join him and saw that the boat was climbing up the side of the canal. A quick peep through the opposite window showed us why ... no water!

During the night, the bottom gate of the next lock had opened and the pound had leaked out, a hazard not unknown; hence the regulation about not mooring in pounds. There wasn't a soul around to help or advise, so we just opened up the paddles of the previous lock and refilled the pound, making sure that the gates of the other lock were shut. However, it was soon obvious that the bottom gates remained shut only when the lock was full, so we had to fill it before we could get enough water in the pound to get the boat upright once more.

With our world the right way up, we could think about breakfast and then I had my master plan for the cats to put into action. Although they both twined themselves around my legs while I prepared our breakfast, I did not feed them. When everything was on the table, I picked up Maple and went to the back of the boat. Owen took Treacle to the front. At a given signal, we quickly opened the doors and deposited the cats on the deck ... not the towpath. Both doors were quickly closed and we sat down to our breakfast.

By putting the cats on the deck, and apart, I knew they would have to explore a bit to find each other. There was so much bird song coming from the hedgerows as the fieldfares were clearing the hawthorn berries that I was sure our two farm-bred hunters would soon find lots of enticing smells to tempt them for a morning's forage, particularly if they found a field mouse or two.

I wanted to look out of the window just to see what was happening, but Owen said let them get on with their breakfast while we got on with ours. Not five minutes had elapsed when Maple's forlorn little face appeared at the window opposite the table; obviously her exploration was the boat itself and she proceeded to walk along the appropriately named cat-walk, a four inch ledge projecting around the whole boat. She stopped and looked at us through all the windows of the room before finishing the circuit and appearing opposite us again.

I wondered if Treacle had gone off on his own as he had not shown up at the windows. Suddenly there was a lot of scuffling and scratching at the front door and we realised that he was still on deck where Owen had put him. We carried on eating and trying not to look up at the window as a little black face pleaded with us.

Then we heard the splash. I rushed to the back door and Owen to the front. Treacle had fallen in. He was swimming between the boat and the towpath and I ran back through the boat to Owen. Just as I reached the

18

front door, Owen staggered back into the boat clutching a bundle of sopping fur that had hurled itself from the towpath on to his chest. I don't know who was wetter, Owen or Treacle. They both smelt pretty awful and both made angry noises. It took two bath towels to mop up Treacle while Owen found himself taking off all the clothing he had put on less than an hour before.

Some six locks later, Treacle repeated his performance. We had stopped for coffee and I decided once again to make the cats leave the boat. It soon became obvious that our problem wasn't the cats running away; quite the reverse.

We continued down the arm, experiencing for the first time travelling at two miles per hour underneath the M1. Just before the motorway the lock presented a double hurdle in the shape of a lift bridge situated immediately outside the lock. So after my battle with the lock gates, I had to swing like Tarzan to open up the bridge before the boat could leave the lock. Then, of course, it was only a matter of tugging down the bridge again, closing the lock gates, pursuing the boat, overtaking it and opening the next lock gates ready for it.

However, all good things (and not so good things) come to an e..d, and at last we finished the locks and had only one lift bridge left. Unfortunately, apparently no one had told the engineer who made it that it should lift up enough to enable a boat to pass underneath. No matter how much I pulled, tugged and swore, I could not raise it more than about two inches.

We were now on the fringe of Northampton, and industry was slowly creeping up alongside. Indeed, a factory was situated by the side of the canal near the bridge. An elderly labourer, seeing my plight, left his pile of boxes and came across slowly.

'Give us yer pole. That'll do it.'

But it didn't. Not until his mate had also come out and heaved with him at the end of the pole, did the timbers start to creak and with the pole supporting the bridge, plus two sweating men at its end, at last we slowly glided by.

Smiling my sweetest, I said, 'thank you so much. I expect you get fed up helping boats through this bridge.

'You're the first boat we've seen for ages.'

I turned to Owen and whispered, 'shall we tell him we'll be back tomorrow?'

'Keep your bloody mouth shut,' came the surprising answer from my beloved as he grabbed the pole back and waved a warm smile and hearty thanks to our rescuers.

I sat in the front well of the boat and watched the red sun reflecting in the windows of houses, factories, warehouses ... we hadn't seen a human being for two days and now we had Northampton in front of us. The exploration was about to begin.

3

We were royally welcomed for our first visit to Northampton. Where the canal joins the River Nene we saw our first signs of wild life; after five miles of open country it was, of all places, outside a brewery that at our approach seven beautiful swans took to the air and preceded us – a truly regal guard of honour.

We passed the glass block monstrosity of a modern brewery and then sadly noticed its old, red-bricked, and now disused predecessor, standing a little further down the river. Empty windows, broken and gaping, brickwork crumbling, but still retaining the lovely lion-headed rings on the river wall, where in days gone by boats had tied up.

The River Nene runs through Beckets Park – Thomas à Becket had his trial in Northampton in 1164 – but immediately before the Park there is a lock. Unlike the canal locks, those on the Nene have gates that go up and down and not in and out, hence their name Guillotine Locks. They also require a different type of lock key, which is obtained from the lock-keeper. He lives in a terraced house, whose garden door opens on to the towpath, not as you would think, by the side of the lock, but quite a way from it, and not very easy to moor near.

We were only going to stay overnight and wondered if we could moor somewhere outside the lock to avoid obtaining a key for this short period. Once again, the relaxed easy manner of the waterways prevailed; not only did the lock-keeper agree to our suggestion but gave us further help. He directed us to the right-hand channel which would take us into the park itself, behind the island where the pleasure boats were stored. 'A nice quiet spot, and safe. You might meet Mr Davis, he looks after the boats. Sometimes comes along to check at night. You just tell him I said you could tie up there.'

Beckets Park was the ideal mooring. The town centre was within easy reach and from the boat we could see the buses, full of shoppers, and workers returning home. Between that hive of activity and us was a beautifully laid out park complete with river and lake. A city park at dusk on a winter's evening had few visitors and we could easily have been in our own garden.

I walked the cats around the park, but they were determined not to lose sight of me. We tried shutting them out once more, but as Treacle fell in for the third time, I knew the experiment was over. The cats would have to go. A sad decision indeed, but it was obvious that they were not at all happy and in fact it would have been cruel to have kept them on the boat.

While the evening meal was cooking, we decided to explore the town. A launderette was top priority as most of the towels had been used up on Treacle! As we left the boat, we noticed that between us and the town was now a dense black area. The park was, of course, unlit, so with our large torch cutting a beam of light ahead, we found our way along paths, across the bridge over the Nene until, coming towards us, we saw another shaft of torchlight.

'That must be the man who looks after the boats,' I said hopefully, not wanting to meet any strangers prowling around in the dark.

Owen went on ahead towards the other torch and as they met, both beams travelled up the respective body. I heard Owen gasp, 'What the hell are you doing here?' 'Looking for you,' came the unexpected reply.

To my amazement, I saw Owen put out his hand and heard shouts of laughter as the two men fell upon each other.

It was Alan, a brilliant jazz pianist whom we had last seen in Wales. What on earth was he doing here in Northampton?

'I'm working for Northampton County Council. I've only been here a couple of months. I read in the local paper about your boat and the piano – thought you might make your first trip here. There's loads of jazz in the town. I've been walking the towpath and park every night after tea for about a week now. My landlady thinks I'm mad ... anyway where is this boat? I've bought along a couple of bottles to launch her, somewhat belatedly.' He swung a carrier bag containing four bottles of Newcastle Brown.

It was about two hours later that we left the boat again, this time to accompany Alan to one of his favourite locals. He had joined us for our evening meal during which Owen caught up with news of who was playing where, and Alan astonished us with names of well known musicians working in the area.

It was almost midnight when we returned to the boat and I was more than ready for my snug, warm bed.

The moment we opened the door I smelt it! It was a rank, acid smell. We stalked into the bedroom, and there, sitting on my pillow, was soft cuddly Maple, and she was wetting all over it!!

One o'clock chimed from a distant church before we had sorted things out. First of all the offending pillow was thrown outside on the deck, then the sheet and quilt cover were changed. Another pillow was brought out from the storage space under the bed and last of all, Owen had to go and change the dirt-box once again. As I closed my eyes, I knew that tomorrow morning I would be making a telephone call to our son to come and collect the cats.

Our one night in Northampton stretched to a week. There was so much to see and do. Jan, our son, arrived the next evening, had dinner, collected the cats and drove them back as a gift to Jill in Hildenborough. Doing more miles in that one journey than we were doing in ten days!

Owen was offered a chance to play with a couple of local bands and I found out that Northampton boasted of a rare thing today; a repertory theatre. And we just had to support that one evening.

Shops and launderette were all to hand and we even went to the swimming baths on a couple of afternoons.

A visit to the local museum took a whole day and I could still have wandered around much longer. Northampton and boots and shoes are synonymous so the museum has a great variety of exhibits covering the history of this trade, including Queen Victoria's wedding shoes, Nijinsky's ballet shoes and some incredible boots made for an elephant in a film about Hannibal.

We were having some trouble with the electrics on the boat and it was decided to change the bank of batteries. We could get only about one hour of electricity a day and on most evenings I was using candles in order to save the power for the water pump. Electricity and water are used very sparingly when you provide your own. We were moored fairly near a mains water tap with which we could fill our 120 gallon tank quite easily. We also used the public toilets in the park and this saved us using our own Elsan. Without the public toilets, we could not have stayed so long as, of course, we depended on the sanitary stations, which are situated alongside canals, to empty and clean our Elsan toilet.

We arranged for a piano tuner to come and check the piano. It not only needed tuning, as its travels by fork-lift truck had knocked it around a bit, but three notes now refused to play.

The piano tuner was delighted to have the opportunity of tuning a piano on a narrow boat. He could not have had a greater contrast as he came to us direct from having tuned the harps and pianos for a symphony concert in the Royal Festival Hall!

It was easy for him to repair the three wrong notes. He simply removed four tin Co-op checks that must have been put into the piano 20 years or so ago when our children were young! The piano's travels had shaken them up and they had fallen between the hammers. How long is it since the Co-op gave up tin checks? We decided to keep the £1 bronze and three tin tokens as souvenirs.

On a last big spending spree I filled all my store cupboards again: a week of entertaining our various guests had depleted our food stocks.

As Owen and I walked home through the park, (for home was definitely what the boat, and Beckets Park had become) carrying our groceries across the bridge, all the lights came on in the large Avon factory which stands on the far side of the park.

The factory is a modern glass block, not my type of architecture at all, but as the offices, staircase and corridors lit up, I suddenly realised how near to Christmas we were. For there, glowing and swinging in all the rooms, were decorations making the whole building look like an illuminated Christmas tree: a perfect farewell present for our last night in Northampton.

After dinner, Owen made a momentous announcement which, if mentioned before we had ordered the boat, would have put me off narrow boats for ever.

'The best thing from now on, is that you should do all the steering at locks, lift bridges ...'

'But,' I started.

'I've given it quite a bit of thought,' he interrupted. 'It's ridiculous when you think about it. There's you, hurling your five feet nothing at lock gates when you could be just standing by the tiller.'

I thought it even more ludicrous that my five feet nothing should try to steer this 65 feet length of steel. Standing by the tiller at the back of the boat, I could just see over the top, and that blue roof went on and on, a long, long way. It was impossible to see the actual nose of the boat and I would have to judge a good five feet of steel in front of where my vision stopped. And to make it worse, if you wanted the boat to point to the right, you swung the tiller in the opposite direction!

'Don't think about the nose; think of the back of the boat. If you put the tiller to the left then the back swings to the left and, of course the nose to the right. It's easy,' was his nonchalant reply to my anxious remarks.

And to my astonishment, it was. The boat responded beautifully although I had the odd nasty moment when lock gates and I seemed to move in the same direction. I discovered how right Owen had been about another thing, that not only surprised me, but was to surprise all newcomers to narrow boats. It is impossible for the steerer to hear anyone speaking from the front of the boat, and sometimes even from the towpath. So, we worked out a sign language which after a few teething troubles worked well. Initial mistakes, as when Owen pointed right and I swung the nose right and immediately smashed the boat into the side of a bridge, caused some blistering remarks between us, as well as scratches to the once pristine boat ... well, why didn't he say he meant the tiller to the right and not the nose?

The 17 locks and the wretched lift bridges were navigated in one go, and as we moored for the night, just after the third bridge, we both realised how much we had learned about our new home since coming along this stretch of water ten days ago. Mind you, Owen had aching shoulders and I suffered from a stiff neck with continually stretching up to see just that little bit more, so that night we went to bed at 8.30 with brandy and coffee.

At about 2 am, I awoke to find Owen in a heavy sweat. He said he felt fine but he was so wet that he had to get out of bed and rub down with a towel. When he got back, however, he started to sweat again so we finished up by sleeping head to toe to give as much space as possible between us and this must have worked as we both remember nothing more until a bright winter sun shone through the gay orange blinds next morning.

4

One of the unlooked for pleasures of our new life was being able to take our time over breakfast. For many years, we had been keen listeners to brief snatches of the Today programme and now we could take our coffee and rolls with ease and listen to as much of the programme as we desired.

We had adapted ourselves quite easily to our new life and had already established a routine. We were usually up by eight with breakfast completed by nine. Washing up was reduced to twice a day to conserve water. Breakfast things were washed with hot water left over from coffee. For the rest of the day, the other dishes and pots were left until after the evening meal, thereby using water from the gas heater only once a day for washing up; electricity was saved by not using the water pump unnecessarily.

While I washed up the breakfast dishes and then read for a spell, Owen practiced on the piano and trumpet daily. We then untied and set off on our travels, never really knowing where we would make our next stop. It might be only a couple of miles before we would see an interesting church, or want to photograph a bridge; or we might continue until lunch-time when a canal pub would tempt us to stop.

The morning that we rejoined the Grand Union Canal at Gayton junction we knew only that we would be turning right and proceeding towards Braunston.

As we turned into the canal we heard a shout, and there running across the British Waterways Board yard and on to the towpath was a young lad. He was waving his arms and shouting to us. Wondering what on earth was wrong, Owen slammed the engine into reverse and I went to the front of the boat. To my surprise, I was handed an envelope, 'I think this is for you,' said the boy. I looked at the address, 'Mr and Mrs Bryce, Grand Union Canal, Bix.'

Yes, it was for us all right. I thanked him and waved as we chugged on. I opened the envelope to discover a Christmas card from Owen's mother. Although we had explained over and over again to her how to get in touch with us, she had obviously not understood. And yet, here we had a Christmas card, posted only three days previously, second-class post, and with a ridiculous address.

A week later, John Timpson read my piece out on the Today programme and as we slowly sipped our coffee, we heard his famous chuckle ho-ho as we praised, for once, the Post Office.

In fact we had worked out a simple method of getting our mail. All our letters were sent to our daughter Linda and also her telephone number was given to the special people who might want us urgently. Every Friday, we rang Linda, told her to which Post Office to send our mail and then we gave ourselves two or three days to reach that particular village or town.

However, to have a card delivered to us in such a personal manner made us feel very special ... we had yet to learn a great deal more about the grapevine of the waterways.

We continued our journey along the Grand Union where, apart from greeting a horse and rider crossing a bridge, we were alone in the world.

We decided to moor at Weedon, which is about eight miles from Gayton. We had had a stop for morning coffee and another for lunch and now at three in the afternoon it was one of those murky winter scenes when dusk and night follow rapidly. And it was so very, very cold. I defy anyone to stand almost motionless at the back of a boat steering hour after hour in bitter cold weather and still be keen on the landscape or even old canal architecture. Everything in its place and at the right time; by now I was more than ready to swop the rural Northampton scenery for a snug, warm cabin.

I knew already that life on the canals wasn't exactly as the books said. In some ways, it could be even better when you lived on them.

Every evening we removed our boating gear and washed, changed into something relaxing, and then a really dry Vermouth while we watched the news on television. After dinner, we would sometimes play cards, read or listen to a selection from the 8,000 tracks on tape we had on board with us. Having our home with us made us feel that we belonged, really belonged, to the canals. No one who just has a few weeks off to 'do 1,000 miles in a couple of months' can really tell you what living on the canal is like. History, yes, they can explain and photograph that, but not day to day life 20th century style. That's what we were hoping to find out.

Early the next morning the canal had an ethereal, pinky mist clinging to it, just like a gauzy transformation curtain used on stage. We were moored to an embankment, high above the village of Weedon. The church stands like a prisoner, closely guarded by the railway on one side and the canal on the other. Here one can see how the railways really did become big brother to the canals.

I went into Weedon to buy milk and eggs and found that although it is set deep in a valley between these two forms of transport, one doesn't get the feeling of being shut in. This is due to the main street being in an L-shape, and the houses themselves are from many different periods.

At the far end of the village stands a huge collection of brick buildings which are now a government office supply depot. Originally they were barracks, built by King George III in case of invasion. He may have been a crazy king, but he knew which place in England was furthest away from any coast when it came to building a retreat for himself.

Weedon has another claim to fame. In a muddy field, close to the canal, the first experiments with radar were carried out in 1935.

The next day, we had a spate of locks to navigate, but we were now using the broad locks, with space enough for two boats at a time. I still had only seven feet of space, however, to enter and leave by as Owen only opened one gate. I could see his point, as it saved him walking right round the lock to open the other gate, and then back again to shut it. We were certainly finding out just how different it was with only two of us instead of having the extra help of a willing holiday crew.

When we reached Long Buckby locks the canal pub looked inviting. It was one of those small, stone buildings with winking brass showing through its windows, and it was also one of the many 'New Inns' dating back some 200 years with which England is scattered.

The mooring was good. The elderly landlady was a truly remarkable character; her part-time barmaid, who lived in a dolls house flat attached to the side of the pub, was extremely friendly and together with the retired waterman, who lived just opposite, they made us so welcome that we stayed for the night. A phone box nearby was another incentive, ready for our weekly call to Linda.

When Owen rang her later that evening, it was to find out that his mother was ill. He decided to return immediately to London to see her. We made enquiries that night in the pub about local buses and trains from Northampton.

The barmaid immediately squashed the idea of catching a bus and called across the bar, 'Charlie, you can take this gentleman into Northampton in the morning can't you?' and within minutes, it was all arranged.

The next morning at seven o'clock, there was Charlie with his car waiting to take Owen into Northampton. Charlie started work at eight but he wasn't at all put out at leaving home extra early just so as Owen could catch the first train.

While Owen was away, I made friends with the people who lived in the tiny toll house at the junction of the Grand Union with the Leicester Arm. They were ex-Salvation Army officers, who had spent most of their life running a school on the canals for the children of the working boat families. They had lived on one boat and used a butty as a schoolroom. Now they lived a secluded peaceful life by the side of the canal. But as they said, 'we'll always miss the boating life and the working boats in particular. It's nice to see the canals used again but it's not the same – it can't be.'

I was to hear a similar comment many times during the next two years, throughout the whole system. One retired waterman, now nearly 80 and still living in a canal cottage near Anderton on the Trent and Mersey, finds it not only astonishing but amusing to see so many people struggling with locks and shallow water as a holiday!

Both Owen and I are great believers in tradition, but we don't believe in going back to a way of life that is so different from today's. Our boat is built on traditional lines, but inside the cabins it has all the modern comforts we can afford. Many people we meet think we are wrong. They tell us we should be living in a boatman's eight feet cabin, but that kind of living would not fit in with what we want to do with our lives. And surely it only suited the early boatman, if it suited him at all, because space was money. They had to live in as small an area as possible in order to carry as much cargo as possible.

We don't earn our living as carriers so we use all our 65 feet space to live in. We happen to want books, radio, typewriters, and tape recorders. They are part of our way of life. And I think we are much truer at heart than the people who want to turn the clock back and build or convert boats that were, after all, designed for a purpose far removed from a week or two's holiday use.

5

It was Christmas Eve and after a drink with our new friends in the New Inn, we went to bed early. The batteries were still not holding their charge and we could only get about two hours of electricity at the end of the day.

We awoke on Christmas morning to find that somehow or other the amount of electricity we had saved overnight, to enable us to use the water pump and to get some light during the dark early hours, had been used up. It was a romantic, if unwashed, candlelit Christmas morning breakfast, and that wasn't the only unusual thing about it.

For the first time in 29 years, there were just the two of us ... no family, no friends. Our home had always been a centre for people to gather at any time of the year, but it was during the Christmas season that friends and all the family met for meals, parties, outings. Of course, being on a farm, it was real Christmas atmosphere, with huge log fires from our own trees, massive meals mainly from home-supplied meat and vegetables and every room decorated with holly, evergreens, berries etc from our own hedgerows. I wouldn't have had it any other way.

And now here we were trying out a completely new idea of Christmas. I hadn't even bought poultry for dinner. We had lamb cutlets and to my own disgust I had bought a Christmas pudding instead of making it. I thought about the family throughout the day and pictured the grandchildren's faces as they opened their presents. I was beginning to agree with Dr Johnson, who said, 'Christmastime is a family time,' and then suddenly we heard the pop, pop, pop of a boat engine and lo and behold, we had neighbours! It wasn't long before we were toasting each other in a welcoming Christmas drink and Ken Greenhaugh and his family from the Manchester area were taking us around their new boat, still unpainted and out for its first trial runs.

By Boxing Day, we felt we had known each other for years and we knew that we would find some excuse to meet up again in the future. We even had an impromptu Christmas party. On Boxing Day, both boats moved off towards Braunston and during lunch time we joined the regulars of the Admiral Nelson, situated by the side of lock number three in the Braunston Locks. We decided it was a suitable place for a farewell drink, as at the junction Ken would be bound towards Rugby while we intended to make for Oxford.

As we opened the door to the bar, opposite us was a piano, on the top of which was a card saying 'pianist wanted'. Owen idly ran his fingers over the keys while waiting for the drinks to be served and that was the beginning of a two-hour playing session with Owen on trumpet and me on piano. After the first few tunes, one of the customers came over to us, took out a pair of spoons from his pocket which he played for the rest of the session.

I seem to mention pubs quite a bit, but the fact is that neither Owen nor I drink much. We love the atmosphere, the people and the gossip, but one glass of sherry or lager is enough for us. So imagine my horror when I noticed lined up on top of the piano, at least six glasses of lager! Happily Ken and his two sons didn't mind helping us to dispose of them.

We said goodbye to our friends on *Commanche* at Braunston and decided to stay a couple of days moored outside the famous Rose and Castle restaurant/pub. Braunston is a real canal centre with a large marina, but you can still see plenty of the old working boats moored here as well.

Helen has her mooring at Braunston. She earns her living from carrying and selling coal up and down the canal and she lives on her boat in a tiny eight feet cabin, a beautifully decorated home with lace plates, highly polished brass, and a cheerful stove. Helen goes also to Leamington Spa to the English Rose Furniture Company to collect all their off-cuts of wood which they are unable to burn or tip. Helen is a well known figure, taking her boat and butty along the canal, full of wood, to the site where she is able to unload it. It's a joy to see her working through locks single-handed; she can close the lock gates without leaving her boat. Boat and butty breast up neatly side by side and stop just at the right time.

Braunston village is still comparatively unspoilt and even the church boasts a feeling of belonging to the canal. By the side of the font stands a boat water-can, which now holds the water for baptising. Funnily enough the gaudy green painted can, with its crude roses running round the sides, doesn't seem out of place in the somewhat austere stone interior of the church.

We had a happy day at Braunston when two musician friends came to tea. Susan plays the piano and her husband, the clarinet. They were both ex-pupils of Owen and had first met at one of his summer schools. Now they were here to christen the music room with Susan on piano, Alex on clarinet, Owen on trumpet, while I poured out the champagne they had brought along.

On the morning of our departure from Braunston I decided to do some last minute shopping in the village and on returning to the boat, I saw that we had neighbours again. This time the boat was a full 72 feet and painted with beautiful panels. I knew that I would like the owner whatever his colour, creed or age because the boat's name was *The Empress of Blandings* and anyone who is a fan of P G Wodehouse is a friend of mine! And I was right – we got on famously. The boat belonged to a master from Christ's Hospital who was spending Christmas with a few friends, also masters from the famous school. When they saw our piano, one of them immediately jumped on board, ran down into the music room and started to play, sight reading from the piece of Scott Joplin ragtime that was on the music stand.

Pure ragtime music as composed by Joplin sounds deceptively simple to play. As a comparatively newcomer to the world of practising musicians, after some 30 years of listening to and studying it, I knew only too well how expert one had to be to make the sounds that were now pouring from the notes of our old piano. I thought how honoured we were to have the music master from Christ's playing on our boat. Then I learned that our virtuoso was the maths master! It was enough to make me want to put a hatchet through the piano for I knew that I'd never sound like that. How unfair I thought, especially when I found out it wasn't even his first choice of a hobby!

To compensate for my chagrin, they invited us on board *The Empress of Blandings* for coffee. It was a really beautiful boat, wood panelling throughout, a marvellous dining table, and a coal fire blazing in the stove. I envied them that! We had decided against solid fuel, as storage for a whole winter would have been a problem and, of course, there was no guarantee that we could have re-stocked when supplies ran low. Calor gas was simple, both in use and storage. We carried three 32 lb cylinders and during the winter months we used an average of one cylinder every five days. *The Empress* although painted in traditional colours and built on traditional lines had the same open plan as us. They had also an extra 20th century invention as I found out when coffee was ready.

Owen had gone to the other end of the boat to have a look at the engine. When the coffee was poured, our host picked up a telephone from the side of the cabin and dialled. A phone rang in the engine room, 'coffee's ready' ... how very civilised.

After lunch, we went our separate ways, we passed the Braunston Turn, on through Lower Shuckburgh and towards Napton on the Oxford Canal.

Napton is a delightful place, with its famous windmill perched high on top of Napton hill as a boaters' landmark for miles in either direction.

To give it the correct name, I should say Napton-on-the-Hill, and the houses, church and school are built on all sides of the hill. The shops and pubs are clustered at the bottom and therefore not many boaters climb the steep road up to the top.

We did, and it was more than worth it on two counts. First, for the view. The panorama of Warwickshire countryside spread like a skirt of many shades of greens and browns, with a pocket of blue and silver glistening from a reservoir or lake, a view our ancestors saw when the canal was first built. Few houses are to be seen, no new developments, no pylons and no main roads. Just sheer beauty. On the way back down the hill, we got our second lucky break. A notice on a farm gate read, 'duck eggs for sale', another rare treat for us. We both love boiled duck eggs for breakfast and had not had any since leaving our own farm.

Oh yes, it's well worth all those Napton locks, and the journey past the depressing brickworks that seem to have millions of bricks lying in untidy piles going to waste, indeed one of their own chimneys has a decidedly dangerous bulge in imminent danger of collapsing onto passing boats at any minute.

It was the last day of 1974 and we did not stay up to see in 1975. We seemed to be really living a back-to-nature life. We got up when it was light and we both felt sleepy by about eight in the evening.

The next morning, I wished Owen a Happy New Year and told him that I had in fact woken up in the night and heard the bells of Napton Church. Owen had done the same thing ... so we had lain side by side wide awake and seen 1975 in after all. What would 1975 bring? Surely no bigger surprise than 1974, for on 1st January 1974 we had never a thought of selling the farm and starting anew.

My new year's wish was that we could sell the farm soon and be completely free at last, for although we were enjoying our boating life, the unsold property was always there, a cloud hanging over our peace of mind.

6

During the next few days, we awoke to bright, but cold sunny mornings with the air crisp, and the whole world around us silent and still. After lighting the gas fires, I would go out into the front well deck to bask in this rare atmosphere of a world belonging only to us, the vast countryside all around and not another soul in sight, often not a house to be seen. The canal was as smooth as silk, the sky reflected in it turning its usual murky brown water into a blue and white picture that was a designer's dream.

The fields had already been ploughed for winter and the sunshine shining on the dew along the smooth sides of the ridges resembled huge blocks of chocolate.

Apart from a lone walker, usually with a dog, we could travel all day and keep the world to ourselves, although sometimes we had the company of a moorhen or mallard, and the occasional flock of fieldfares, busily gorging on hawthorn berries in the hedges.

I've always known that I was a late developer and I was to prove it even more during the next few months. Fancy getting to the age of 49 before seeing your first kingfisher, and even a few months older before recognising pee-wits and finding out the difference between a yellow wagtail and a grey one.

My bible during that first year on board *Bix* was the *Book of British Birds*. It became very well thumbed day after day as we slowly moved along. I'd hear a piercing whistle, or a small piping note and rush down into the boat, grab the book and the binoculars and start feverishly looking into the hedgerows, back to the book, up into the trees, back to the book. As the months went by, I realised how lucky I was to start my serious bird-watching in the winter. No leaves on the trees. How frustrating it is in spring and summer to hear all that activity and see so little.

It was at Cropredy that we made human contact again, a quiet place that was ideal for our re-awakening to the world about us. The lock-keeper's wife was planting some daffodil bulbs and we had a 'gardeners' chat while passing through the lock. We both agreed that January was a bit late to put out daffs, but it seemed better to put them in the soil than keep them in the garden shed, where they had been pushed to the back of a shelf and forgotten.

The lock and canal side at Cropredy are very pretty and well cared for, and the towpath has recently been re-surfaced. Unfortunately, the British Water Board use the most wretched of stones as the material for this work. These are not small enough for your foot to cover as you step on them and not large enough to avoid. They are a medium-sized, many-edged, lethal

Iris Bryce and her husband Owen, relax on board *Bix*

The piano finds a new home. Anxious moments as it is loaded into *Bix*

Iris discovering new muscles

After dinner entertainment

A visit to the Waterways Museum at Stoke Bruerne, Northants

Kitchen chores

weapon on which my soft soled boating shoes are useless. To jump off a boat on to such a surface is excellent practice for any fakir who has forgotten his bed of nails.

The seam at the back of one of my deck shoes had been ripped, making the shoes no longer waterproof. However, even a small village like Cropredy has a hardware store where we bought some rubber solution. We bought more in several other villages also, but sad to say none of them worked on my shoes and even after two years of various kinds of glue, adhesives and plastics, I still have one leaky shoe.

We were still having trouble with the electricity on the boat and after another phone call to the boatyard, it was decided that an electronics expert should be called in. Tony arrived a day or so later when we were near Fenny Compton. At first, the cause of our troubles seemed to mystify him: the batteries were OK and were charging correctly, but somewhere there must be a leak. Eventually, it was found. The alternator behind the ignition was faulty and permanently in the 'on' position, using up electricity even when we had switched off the ignition.

A larger alternator was recommended and it was decided that the boat should go into Tony's own yard to have this work done and, of course, to have the other fault rectified.

And so we gave up our original idea of reaching Oxford and went only as far as Banbury. After so much beautiful cruising through peaceful waters, quiet hamlets, and lush countryside, it came as a shock to find ourselves sharing the water with mounds of rubbish, floating debris of mattresses, cardboard boxes, enormous tree trunk-like pieces of wood and thick sluggish water.

Banbury, of course, is famous for the spicy Banbury cakes, and every child knows that 'if you ride a cock horse to Banbury Cross, you'll see a fine lady upon a white horse'. Alas, not today, for Banbury's streets, like most of those in England are now the prerogative of the motor car. Even the 17th century nursery rhyme cross has been pulled down and replaced by a 19th century replica.

However, you can still eat the delicious cakes that Ben Johnson wrote about in his *Bartholomew Fair*, published in the 17th century. And it did my heart good to see a splendid Victorian post box in the town centre which, according to the plaque beside it, had been re-erected after petitions to the Post Office by the local inhabitants. Hurrah for the present day Banbury folk.

When it came to the canal part of Banbury, we were less happy. First and foremost, there were those terrible lift bridges. There are the Banbury kids on hand to help you, but this is mostly in summertime. In winter, when the mud in the ruts has caked into a cement-like consistency and there's only one pair of hands to pull, shove, tug, heave and haul, then it's sheer torture.

By the time we fought the first two and left a queue of Saturday afternoon drivers furious at being delayed (only one actually got out to help Owen), we decided that we'd turn at the next winding hole which was on the edge of the town. This still gave us easy access to shops but avoided two more lift bridges and a lock.

It was at this point that we found out that a guide book is only as good as its latest revision. Our waterways guide was newly bought, but when we reached our turning point, it just wasn't there. We would have had trouble with a canoe, let alone 65 feet. A boatyard nearby was a mixture of museum pieces and plain rubbish, some of the old wooden narrow boats had years of growth of grass and sedges coming out of the sides. However, the owner of the yard was as kind and helpful as he could be. We bought some diesel from him and as Owen helped him lift the five gallon drums across the yard, over the sinking hulls, and then precariously poured the fuel through a dilapidated funnel, the old man had explained that no boat had turned around here for years. Our so-called 'new' guide was very obviously well out of date and we had to go through the next two lift bridges and the lock, before we could turn the boat around.

I wrote that night to the publishers and offered to revise their maps as we went on our journeys. Their reply was 'yes, please'. I wrote back asking about a fee. They replied just as quickly, 'we don't pay anything; we depend on holiday-makers to write in and tell us.' So that's why some books are so very, very full of mistakes!

There was, however, a very happy moment for us in Banbury. During our weekly phone call, the estate agents informed us that someone had made an offer for the farm. Owen was in the phone box while I stood outside. He opened the door and said, 'we've been offered £29,000'. 'Let's take it,' I said. He nodded and as we returned to the boat we were both in a very thoughtful mood.

What a drastic decision – to sell property valued at £45,000 for £29,000. But was it? It had now been on the market for almost a year but, we worked out, that even with this enormous drop, we would still have enough to invest in the small cottage or house where we would finally settle.

Even in our remote existence on the canals inflation had made itself known. We hadn't actually bought a national newspaper for 25 years or more, the BBC news had shown it would help if we didn't touch the interest on whatever was left over to invest – a balance to inflation if you like.

And we still had the £25 per week coming in from our loan to the small company in which we had shares and on which it had proved quite easy for us to live.

The light on our personal horizon was certainly brighter once the contracts for the sale were under way. To make our stay in Banbury even more enjoyable, I found a launderette that actually backed onto the canal and what's more advertised the fact on its back wall. What a wonderful convenient stop-over for us boating types.

So with the galley cupboards well stocked and our clothes washed and ironed, it was time to gird our loins and face the lift bridges again as we retraced our route along the Oxford Canal to Foxton and the electronics wizard who was to restore our electricity supply.

7

Our return along the Oxford Canal was as quiet and uneventful as the outward one. Most days, I shouted to cows in the fields alongside and they sometimes stopped chewing, to gaze mournfully at the boat; and on some days we saw a couple of fishermen sitting patiently, rod in hand, staring glassily into the water.

After a couple of fruitless attempts, I gave up exchanging greetings as no one bothered to answer, except one man who shouted angrily, 'you're well out of season aren't you?' It was to be months before we actually got a nod and a smile from an angler – even though we always slowed down when passing them.

As we approached Fenny Compton tunnel we saw, to our surprise, another boat coming towards us. It was about three o'clock and the mist was creeping down the steep sides of the deep cutting we were cruising through. Fenny Compton tunnel belies its name. The tunnel was opened up several years ago and now boats chug through a narrow, deep cutting wide open to the skies, but it's still known as Fenny Compton Tunnel. The high road bridge crossing the canal rose suddenly out of the mist, the iron railings curving along its side seeming to lead straight into the heavens.

Although visibility was poor, we could see that it was a boat in front of us, but it just did not seem to be moving. Slowly we drew nearer but still could see no one at the tiller although now it did look as if the boat was coming towards us. Fog plays all sorts of queer tricks with eyesight and I wondered if I'd conjured up a vision of a ghost boat. But, yes, it was a real boat and it was moving, just, and there wasn't a soul at the tiller. The mist surrounded us now and it was bitterly cold. I simply hoped that we would manage to get past the boat and tie up quickly for the night. A sudden shout alerted both Owen and me and we saw, standing on the towpath, shrouded in the mist a young man. He was pulling a rope and we realised that he was in fact hauling his boat by hand.

As we drew closer we saw that he was exhausted, and no wonder. The contraption he was pulling was a full 70 foot working boat that had been half converted while the other half contained an assortment of engines, an old bicycle, and pots and pots of paints and varnishes. Even the one time cabin was minus its rear wall which now supported a canvas sheet.

As it was impossible to pass, we tied up against this floating museum piece and made some tea. It was then we heard his tale of woe. No job; he had decided to buy this boat, take it to a mooring in Oxford, do it up and sell it. There was only one snag: the engine had virtually disintegrated on the second day and now the only way to get it to the mooring was to tow or bow haul it as was the practice in the early days on the canals.

There was little we could do to help, except warm him up a bit and fill his splendid old fashioned, extremely heavy metal Thermos flask with boiling water. Before we continued our separate ways, he asked us to pass on his troubles to any boat going his way so that they would look out for him and perhaps give him a tow.

Sad to say, we saw no other boat for three weeks and by then we were far from the Oxford Canal.

To get to the boatyard at Foxton, we had to return almost to Buckby where we had spent Christmas and here we turned off the Grand Union and went along the Leicester section. The first mile is through beautiful woods where you are lulled into a serenity that is rudely shattered when you approach the Watford Staircase locks.

These were our first staircase locks so we moored overnight at Norton Junction, the beginning of the Leicester section, to be fresh in the morning to face the arduous challenge of seven locks. They really are like stairs, one lock leading direct into the next, so that the top gate of the first lock is the bottom of the second, and so on, right up the flight.

We awoke to a blustery winter morning with grey heavy skies, and what was, for the canal, fairly choppy water.

The first lock has a bridge immediately outside it and as we approached so the wind roared along the canal and swung us round. It was our first day all over again, only this time we had the bridge to navigate before the lock gates.

After 15 minutes' struggle to prevent the boat demolishing the bridge, Owen decided that I should jump off at the nose and stand at the foot of the bridge, holding the front rope taut while he manhandled the tiller and boat into the lock.

Have you ever stood on a six-inch stone ledge trying to hold 14 tons of steel while a force eight gale persuades it the opposite way and, to add to your troubles, a cloudburst descends from immediately overhead? Finally we managed the first lock of the staircase whereupon it was much easier to operate the locks than the complicated notices alongside suggested. Even the continuous rain didn't matter after a while, but when eventually we emerged from the top lock, number seven, we went no further than the M1 motorway bridge, beneath which we moored for a break and shelter.

By late afternoon we had reached the village of Crick with our self-esteem much restored thanks to the incident related below which made us feel we were now accepted as a small part of the waterways.

Before reaching Crick, you have to pass through a tunnel. Canals have many tunnels, some short, no more than the width of a bridge, others two miles in length. It's always with trepidation that you enter a tunnel with its long black interior and the pinhole of light way, way down at the end, the constant drip of water from the walls and often a sudden torrent of cold water from an air shaft. However, our *Bix* had been built just outside the longest tunnel now navigable, Blisworth tunnel, through which we had taken the boat several times on trial runs: after that two-mile marathon, the 1,500 yards of Crick tunnel was no hazard.

As we approached the tunnel, we were confronted by a group of British Waterways Board workmen awaiting a boat to tow their butty through. It contained scaffolding to be erected at the other end of the tunnel where repairs were in progress.

They were surprised to see us chugging along on this wet January afternoon, but the foreman was quick to ask if we could tow their butty through the tunnel to which, of course, we said, 'yes'. We'd save them quite a bit of time, they told us, and as we started off the foreman jumped into his van to go ahead by road and tell the working party at the other end to be ready for us.

We emerged to cheers and thanks, and as we slipped the tow rope we knew we had made a few more friends along the canal.

After tying up at Crick, we went for a walk around the village, spotting one or two interesting looking buildings tucked away down a little street at the top of the narrow main road, but nothing else to make us want to walk around for long on such a wet and miserable afternoon. And then, almost as if to say sorry for such a rotten day, mother nature gave us the most spectacular sky that either of us had ever seen. We stood at the top of the High Street and watched the dark clouds fade into a mother of pearl silver, then quietly, as if He had turned up the dimmer switch, brilliant streaks of green and mauve thrust fingers of iridescent shimmers, which as if by magic turned themselves into a purple-pink glow, and then as the huge red ball of the sun appeared, the entire sky burst into flame. We must have stood transfixed on the pavement, outside the Co-op, for at least a quarter of an hour, not speaking, while shoppers pushed by in and out of the supermarket. Could they not see all that glory above and around them? Why did it affect us in such a way and not them? At last, shivering as the sun began to fade and slip down the sky, we turned and went back down hill towards *Bix*. As we clambered down the steps into the cabin, there hanging on its hook was the camera ... put there to remind us to take it with us when we went out. Once again we had remembered it too late.

Next morning we moved on to Yelvertoft, a quiet hamlet with a population of 500 or so and even though it does have a wide main street, I'm sure we could have sat down in the middle of it in safety, for we saw not a single car while there.

We were to find the Leicester section full of surprises for although it is itself an arm leading off the main Grand Union Canal, it in turn has two arms leading off again. The first one is a little more than a mile long and leads to the village of Welford.

We had a delightful mooring on the Welford arm, and England's weather being what it is, on the 16th January, 1975, we cruised along under brilliant blue skies with the sun warm on our backs; above us gliders gracefully competing in aerobatics with the gulls.

There were quite a few boats moored in the basin at the end of the Welford arm and we could imagine how popular this part of the canal must be in the summer. It is here that you negotiate Welford lock, one of the smallest locks on the system, dropping no more than a few inches.

After lunch we made our way towards North Kilworth, just far enough to travel before these early winter nights start. Thanks to the shallow water, we found it impossible to get the boat near enough to the bank to tie up. We moved on a little further and then a little more. Now it began to get dark and for the first time we realised that we might have to travel in the dark before finding a mooring. Obviously to jump off a boat in an unknown and unlit place could be dangerous.

Our map told us that Husbands Bosworth tunnel was not far away. Although it is only 1,200 yards long, we did not fancy passing through it to emerge into a black night scene perhaps with still no suitable mooring. There are usually places, however, just outside tunnels where boats can wait while another craft comes through the tunnel, but at Husbands Bosworth even this spot was too shallow. Owen decided to try the opposite bank, a steep embankment covered in bramble and hawthorns. The boat drew closer and closer. 'Jump,' he ordered and I did just that, off into the dark void in front of me. I landed in soft mud and felt my legs sinking deeper and deeper. I became terrified. I could see nothing. The spotlight on the boat was pointing dead ahead into the tunnel: all around me was a soft black nothing.

I started to panic until Owen came up to the front of the boat and held out the pole ... but even then the situation turned into a nightmare as I grabbed and slipped back, grabbed again, until finally I found that extra surge of strength and lifted myself up, holding tight to the pole. Slowly the mud released its hold on my legs, when I thankfully grabbed the side of the boat and clambered over into the front well deck. In fact the boat was quite close in and Owen, by the light of our torch, managed to secure us to a couple of saplings. Meanwhile the nose of the boat was almost in the mouth of the tunnel and through the night we could hear the drip, drip of the water as it fell from the tunnel roof. Not a mooring to be recommended.

After a shower and a change of clothes, I sat before the fire giving serious thought to what we had done; we had given up our lovely farm, moved away from friends and family and taken to a roving boating life. My legs ached. Surely I was past the age for jumping on and off boats, pulling and heaving ropes. I was a grandmother; why not behave like one?

And then, Owen came and sat by my side. He had two glasses of brandy in his hands and the waterways map under his arm. He smiled gently at me, 'Here, drink this down, you deserve it.' I took it gratefully as he went on, 'thought I'd read up about the Foxton Staircase locks; we shall be there tomorrow about lunchtime, I reckon. Did you know there's ten of them – that's even more than Watford. I've got to get you ready for that little lot haven't I?'

I started to giggle ... he thought it was the brandy ... I knew that my questioning thoughts were running away.

8

Foxton is a mecca for canal enthusiasts, and all because of the Foxton Inclined Plane, an alternative to the Foxton Staircase Locks, built in 1900 and closed 11 years later. It carried two boats up one side and two down the other on a counter balance system, or that is how it was designed. Alas, mechanical faults were numerous and running costs high until eventually it was abandoned, the locks coming back into their own again.

But people still come to visit Foxton and to stare at the steep slope with the rails partly visible through weeds and undergrowth, where the mud, that is, allows weeds to grow.

At Foxton, we had a lucky break, for as we started through the locks a party of school children arrived for a social history lesson about the local canal system – and what better way to learn than to help work a boat through them!

With our eager young assistants, we took about 50 minutes to get through the 10 locks. Of course, it rained all the time, but no one minded and it was cups of hot coffee all round at the end. Well, not actually cups, my crockery wasn't planned for a party of 20 so it was mugs, glasses, tooth mug and a small jar originally potted by my daughter for my yoghourt.

We stayed at Foxton for a day to attend to our electrical troubles: snow and a frozen canal greeted us the following morning as we made towards Market Harborough. Within minutes, I was frozen, fingers numb inside two pairs of mittens and feet, despite insulated socks inside wellington boots, were angrily protesting.

The Market Harborough arm, thankfully, is lock-free but it does have a swing bridge which stubbornly refused to live up to its name, even though we had two little boys, on their way to violin lessons, four fishermen, one mum with two toddlers, plus Owen of course, all of them pushing and tugging to open it. When our helpers totalled 14, we saw it move, inch by inch until there was room enough for me to scrape the boat through. Then we had the same job closing it! Will there ever be a swing bridge that swings, or a lift bridge that lifts, without the strength of superman being required?

The canal had a sugar-frosted look all day and the ropes froze to the deck. As *Bix* forced her way through the veneer of ice which covered the canal, it made the most tremendous booming noise echoing throughout the length of the boat.

We journeyed all day with only one stop – for lunch. We met no other boats, but did see two boys fishing during the afternoon. I couldn't help wondering why their fingers weren't frozen to their rods; I could hardly feel mine and yet they were not even wearing gloves. I wanted to reach Market Harborough for some urgent laundering as we had not found a convenient launderette since Banbury and I'd been forced to wash the smalls by hand aboard. Drying was the difficulty: I usually finished by putting the clothes around the fire which increased the condensation in the lounge. And who likes to relax at night with a clothes-horse of wet clothes staring you in the face?

The canal arm ends abruptly in a basin which is occupied by a boatyard so we moored where the canal merges into the basin. A storm blew up to greet us, making mooring very difficult; to make matters worse we had to use the gang-plank as the canal was so shallow.

We were blown and buffeted all night as the storm raged overhead. We could hear our television aerial and cable swinging and creaking; the boat itself swung viciously as the wind raced over the water slapping the water against the side up to our bedroom window.

Next morning we learned another lesson: always bring in the gang-plank at night. Ours was missing and we were actually untied at the stern and lying across the canal.

Owen had arranged to visit his mother, who was now in hospital in Hertfordshire, and his train left Market Harborough at 7.30 am. So with an anorak over the top of my nightdress, and wearing wellington boots and a madly gay red plastic rain hat, I helped to pole the boat back to the towpath. It was 6.30 am, pitch black and the rain still fell. Eventually we managed to get near enough for Owen to jump off and secure the boat.

As he disappeared into the gloom, he said it would be easy to find the plank in daylight as it had probably just floated into the basin. He did not tell me how I was going to get off a boat that was some four foot from the bankside.

It was too dark to look for the plank and it was still raining, but I knew it would clear up in time for me to find the local launderette. You see, my old Dad had developed a good weather eye during his 50-odd years as a Thames barge-builder and he had taught us that, 'rain before seven: fine before eleven', all to do with the tide turning, I believe. It was only seven now, as I sat munching hot buttered rolls.

By nine o'clock, the sky had lost its leaden look and turned a gauzy, milky grey. The rain was down to a fine drizzle and I packed the launderette bag. It was a heavy load as almost all the double wincyette sheets had been used up, plus pillowcases, towels and both the duvet covers.

I surmounted the problem of having no gang-plank by paddling through about 18 inches of water, with my trousers rolled up, my boots tied round my neck. Drying my feet and legs on one of the dirty towels I was soon on my way to the town of Market Harborough.

It's not a convenient town for boaters as the shopping centre is quite a distance from the mooring, but the spectacular spire of St Dionysius's Church beckons you and once beneath the graceful iron inn sign of the Swan, you haven't far to go.

I noted the supermarket, cheese shop and greengrocer where I would return to restock on my next expedition, but as I travelled up one side of the high street and down the other, I had a feeling that one of my nightmares had come true: I had landed in a town without a launderette.

Eventually, I asked some shoppers, but they shook their heads. I stopped a policeman and he confirmed my suspicion. As I walked away, he stopped me and said he did remember one on a Council estate about two miles outside the town. He called up a colleague on his walkie-talkie to check if it was still open and then gave me directions on how to walk to it ... no, there were no buses going that way. And in fact, I found out some five minutes later that the one-time bus station was shut and looked like the backdrop to a ghost town western.

It was just three o'clock that afternoon when I returned to the boat, arms half pulled out of their sockets after carrying the laundry nearly six miles in all. Now, all I had to do was to find a way back aboard the boat. In daylight, I could see that we still had a few feet clear behind us so I untied the boat and pulled it back and back until the stern deck was almost level with the edge of the basin. My arms now no longer belonged to my body at all, but at least I could step straight onto the back of the boat.

As I bent down to pick up the laundry bag from beneath a tree I heard a peculiar noise above my head. There was a starling and from its mouth dangled a nylon fishing line, the other end tangled around the branches of the tree.

Although it squawked and screamed at me, I managed to climb up the tree and get hold of the bird and found inside its throat a coloured float attached to the fishing line. Obviously, the bird had been attracted by the bright red and yellow object and tried to eat it.

I went back on board *Bix* and with a sharp knife and my kitchen scissors managed to cut through the wire between bird and tree, but this still left the bit down its throat. Most of it came away, but at the last moment the small float disappeared down the bird's throat. It shook its head, opened and shut its mouth a few times, and when I tried to look down inside its mouth, it promptly bit me and flew away.

So it was nearer to four o'clock by the time I got my clean washing home, the kettle on, and my soaking hat and coat hung away. Oh yes, I was wet all right: the drizzle of the morning had developed into a thunderous downpour during my walk to the launderette and back. Perhaps, my dad's weather lore referred only to the Thames ... after all there are no tides on the canal.

When Owen returned very late that night, he was surprised to see that I had not found the plank. What on earth had I been doing all day? I didn't answer. I was too busy filling up a mail-order coupon for a folding bicycle. In fact I ordered two.

The silver lining in the grey clouds came our way when we collected our mail next morning, for much to our delight we received the final confirmation of the sale of the farm. Three days later, we took turns to sign a cheque for £8,000, the balance due on the boat. With great pleasure we walked to Peter Ellis's office in Market Harborough and handed it over. I'm sure that he too shared our relief in paying off this debt, for by now we had been on board *Bix* for almost three months.

Our plank turned up too. It was found floating between the hire boats in the basin. At last, with a full, clean linen cupboard and a restocked galley, it was time to start off on our travels again. This time, with instructions from a Waterways Board employee, of all people, about 'that bloody swing bridge. You're going the right way this time to give it a ram with your boat, that'll start the bugger off,' he said.

9

It was the season of long dark nights and short cold days. We went to bed early and got up much later than we had done for several years. Very few television programmes held our interest for long and those that might have done were obviously more suitably timed for all-night watchmen than anyone else. We read, wrote, played Scrabble, Mastermind, and cards. I started some enamel-painting. Owen rerecorded lecture tapes, played the piano and trumpet. The days passed peacefully in a world far removed from telephones, traffic, queues and many other modern-day amenities that were once a part of our everyday life. It was a bit of a shock to realise suddenly, as I feverishly searched at the back of the food cupboard, that the last of the coffee had been used. A further look showed a very depleted store indeed.

Incredible as it sounds, we were only about ten miles from Market Harborough but we had taken nearly two weeks to cover this distance. The canal had been taking us through remote, rural country which had relaxed and lulled us into an almost perpetual day dream.

By the time we reached Saddington, I was using dried milk powder which I did not care for. This small village is perched high on a hill and the road leading from it to the canal was like a wind tunnel on the morning we toiled up and up towards our fresh supply of groceries. Almost bent double, with our breath being sucked out of us as the wind tore at our clothing, we trudged up the hill, the thought of fresh milk and vegetables driving us on.

Our guide book informed us we would find a post office, telephone and stores but as we roamed the village streets and lanes, we realised too late that it was another one of its jokes. We did find the post office, and the postmistress was very apologetic as she leant over the wooden flap which came down across her hall-way, turning the rear part of her passage into the 'shop.' 'I'm ever so sorry, we only sell stamps and postal orders and things like that. Milk? Oh no, we have to get ours from Fleckney, over the next hill.'

Ah well, it's tinned veg, a one-last-egg omelette between us, a chocolate flavoured mould made with that dreadful powdered milk ... actually our evening meal tasted better than it sounds. I wondered, as I ate it, why the guide book bothered to tell us Saddington's early closing day.

A further four and a half miles along the canal was Newton Harcourt, a well known local beauty spot favoured by the inhabitants of Leicester. We would obviously get supplies there as the place catered for visitors.

Before reaching this rather spread-out village, we had to go through Saddington tunnel. As I had yet to take the boat through a tunnel Owen thought it a good idea if I had a go at this one.

43

Nervous at first, I soon found myself hypnotised as I watched the headlight of the boat pierce the darkness and make ever increasing circles of light shine on row after row of curving bricks climbing up the walls and over the roof. The pinhole of daylight at the end of the tunnel that was my target, held its shape for what seemed hours, and then suddenly it grew larger and larger, until the greens of the grasses and the watery sunlight caused me to blink like a mole emerging from the earth.

Owen congratulated me on my steering. I hadn't hit the wall on either side once! He wondered if the bats had worried me. Bats? Yes, didn't I know that Saddington tunnel was famous for its bat population? Naturalists enthuse over the numbers living there. I hadn't seen one, and I'm not surprised, because Owen's information came from that same guide book!

We reached Newton Harcourt after lunch and the guide book was right at last. There was a post office and there was a shop. We could fill our cupboards with as much as we liked, as long as it was beer, spirits, wine or minerals, and if we waited until 6 pm. The one and only shop was an off-licence!

Dinner that evening was the last rubbery carrot, grated with some milled peanuts and mixed with mayonnaise, rice cooked with the last tin of tomatoes and pancakes made with flour, powdered milk, no egg and filled with the scrapings from the marmalade pot.

It must sound strange in the day of the motor car and modern shopping precincts to have to relate that, although we were on the outskirts of Leicester, such was the remoteness of the canal that our food supply situation was getting quite serious. I had plenty of flour and dried yeast and could still make bread but I had precious little else.

The next morning, we reached paradise in the shape of one of those corner shops that sell everything. It's not mentioned in the guide book, but it's near Wigston and I beamed a happy smile as I spent a small fortune inside. The proprietor was a character, a non-stop talker, wisecracking with all his customers who obviously knew him intimately. His windows were covered with painted slogans advertising his wares and for the first time I saw 'wholemeal bread' splashed across a window in white paint.

Blaby was the next town the canal passed through and to my delight it boasted a good variety of shops and a launderette. Blaby is a suburb of Leicester, so we decided to take a bus into the city and have a look around. Our purchases included a large tin of silica-gel crystals to be used to combat dampness in our piano, stereo, books etc. I had made several small linen bags and we planned to put one bag of silica-gel into each piece of equipment, and change it weekly. The dry crystals turn pink when damp and I had only to put the bags into the gas oven at a medium heat for 20 minutes whereupon they dried out, turning back to blue again.

We spent a long time exploring the Jewry Museum in which I was greatly intrigued by a piece of Roman graffiti that, translated, read, 'Lucinda the actress loves Claudius the gladiator' so much better than the banal slogans with which the paint spray addicts boringly cover the canal bridges.

Owen suggested that we stay in Leicester for a slap-up meal to celebrate the sale of the farm and we decided on the Grand Hotel. Before booking a table, we thought it wise to find out the time of the last bus back to Blaby. It sounds simple enough but first find your bus station. We walked through the city, round the city and across the city, then suddenly we saw the street we wanted – but no, it only looked like it. We asked the way and were directed back whence we had come. This time we turned down a street we had missed and there was the bus station. But not ours. 'No,' said the Inspector. 'Go back until you come to the Armoury, you know the ruin in the middle of the road, then take the second on the left.' We did and there was the bus station. But not ours. An hour later, we found out that lucky old Leicester has five bus stations – ours of course was number five.

I was too worn out to contemplate eating anything by now and all I wanted was to get back to the boat. But Owen dismissed the idea promptly. 'There are plenty of buses up to 11 o'clock. You'll feel fine after a relaxing glass of sherry.'

As we entered the brilliantly-lit foyer of the Grand Hotel and were luxuriously surrounded by its velvet and warmth, I became conscious of the old anorak, winter boots and bright woolly hat I was wearing. They were out of place beside the bejewelled evening-gowned females who were emerging from the ladies cloakroom powdered and perfumed, ready for an annual ladies night banquet.

I ignored their surprised looks as I joined them and washed my somewhat grimy hands in preparation for my night out.

We had a wonderful meal in the downstairs restaurant. Deep, comfortable, red velvet settees and chairs, a real waiter from the old school, who looked after us like an anxious father. Was the food to our liking? And the wine? He didn't hover, was not in the least simpering, and did not push himself into the conversation. He was truly anxious to ensure that we had a good meal and enjoyed ourselves. It was wonderful to be pampered, and how rare to see someone really enjoying his work.

Too soon, it was time to brave the cold wintry night and return to our floating home. Unbelievably, our bus station was at the bottom of the same street in which the Grand Hotel dominated the top corner. *Bix*, we realised, was our only home now ... the farm was well and truly sold.

We got off the bus and walked down by the side of the bridge and there was *Bix* shining in the moonlight. But what on earth were those two white oval things bobbing around in the water at the back of it? As we drew closer, we saw with great delight that we had two swans fast asleep with their necks tucked well into their wings. What better ornaments to set off one's home?

10

I learned a new word as we approached Leicester by boat – 'canalised.' It is used to describe what happens when a river meets and joins with a canal. Outside Leicester, the River Soar joins the Grand Union Canal, thereby canalising the river.

This wide stretch of water, flanked by impressive broad paths, should make an imposing entrance to the city itself. It should, but it doesn't; the reason being today's accumulation of rubbish, litter and filth that seems to accompany human beings in work and leisure alike. For the first time since Banbury we again brushed sides with old car seats, tyres and, believe it or not, dozens of discarded Christmas trees. At one lock, we had to push a car seat and a railway sleeper along with our boat pole to prevent their jamming the gates.

Does Leicester have a municipal tip? Surely it must take people considerable time and effort to transport a Christmas tree or old settee to a canal and tip it in? The amount of domestic items bobbing along in the water or sticking in the mud is far more than can be blamed on the householders living by the canalside.

However, we found a pleasant mooring close to the city centre. We tied up behind St Margarets Church, and the attractive green open space lived up to its name of St Margaret's Pastures. Opposite us, on the other side of the canal was an engineering factory, but we didn't find this unpleasant, quite the opposite as we awoke to a rose-cachou aroma emanating from it which hung in the air for the rest of the day, giving an impression of living near a Turkish harem!

Our mooring was convenient also for a visit to BBC Radio Leicester. I had been a regular contributor to Radio Medway before leaving Kent and my producer had suggested I pop into local radio stations on my travels and see if they would be interested in any scripts. We were lucky in Leicester, for not only did we fix an appointment for a talk to take place on board *Bix*, but Owen found that an old colleague from Broadcasting House in London was now the assistant station manager, and that very night Owen was back in Leicester's studios taking part in a jazz programme.

We spent five happy days in Leicester before setting off towards Loughborough. The scenery immediately changed to flat water meadows on either side of us and we felt as if we were really on a river instead of a canal; but once again we were soon boating through a great deal of floating rubbish.

As we slowly cruised past Syston, an elderly man walking with his dog along the towpath suddenly waved his arms, pointed to the front of the boat and shouted something to me. If you have ever stood at the back of a 65 foot narrow boat, with the engine rumbling beneath your feet, you'll know that it's impossible to hear anyone from the towpath.

The pointing and shouting continued and I yelled to Owen who was down below to go forward and see what was the matter. I reversed the engine to slow down, because the old gent was so agitated, apprehensive that something was wrong up forward. As we slowed and drifted into the side, Owen leaned over and started talking to the old man. They both laughed and then waved to each other. Owen turned and gave me the signal to carry on. By now, the nose of the boat was well and truly into the bank and the stern was coming along side as well. I had to pole off the back before getting under way. Owen emerged grinning. That's the first of them,' he said. 'He's a jazz fan and wanted to know, if we'd called the boat after his favourite trumpet player Bix Beiderbecke.' Not for the first time in my life, I found myself cursing a jazz fan ... why on earth did he have to behave so ridiculously? I then realised what a surprise it must have been to him; after all we jazz followers are still in a minority.

We continued through countryside almost entirely given over to quarries, a very attractive pink stone coming from one at Mount Sorrel. After this stretch, the canal became rather dismal as we approached Loughborough, where the faceless wall of the Herbert Morris factory greets you and goes on and on and on.

Loughborough itself, however, does have an unusual feature: a carillon tower where performances are given throughout the year, sad to say not whilst we were there. The tower stands in Queens Park, a colourful place even in the winter. In the summer, it must be a riot of colour for not only are there flower beds and a variety of shrubs and trees, but the railings are multi-coloured, gaily painted in blue, yellow and red and to top it all there is an aviary of exotic feathered birds ... it was the first time I had seen a navy blue bird.

We stayed only a day in Loughborough as it was so cold. Next morning, still bitterly cold, we started off again. About a mile from the town, we spotted a water standpipe and decided to top up. During the winter months, some water points are turned off as a precaution against frost. This tap, however, was adjacent to a boat yard and still in use, but we did have some difficulty in getting our hose over the tops of the boats which were moored near the tap. I held one end of the hose, which just reached the top of our filling hole and Owen managed to fix the other end to the tap. Taps have different pressures and most we had found run on the slow side. I stood by to check that the water was in fact running into our tank and Owen turned on the tap. WHOOSH! It came with the force of Niagara and our hose somersaulted out of the tank and turned itself on to me – full frontal. Owen yelled that I should have wedged it in more securely but my teeth were chattering too much for me to answer. It meant a complete change of top clothing as well as socks since the water had streamed into my wellington boots.

To compensate for my misery at lunch time we ate out, stopping at a pub

47

conveniently situated on the side of the canal at Normanton. Pubs on canals are rarer than on rivers we had found.

After lunch, we went through Kegworth Locks. There are two, the shallow one and the deep one and, of course, it was as we entered the deep lock that our throttle cable snapped, and the boat just went on and on into the lock where it crashed to a stop after hitting the front gate.

Neither Owen ashore operating the lock nor I on the boat knew that the cable had snapped. All I knew was that the engine failed to respond when I put it into reverse. From Owen's viewpoint, I had probably left it too late to stop the boat and he yelled down at me to pay more attention to steering.

After a furious shouting match, when I would have willingly given the boat to the first person to turn up, we checked the cause of the trouble and found the cable broken. There was not much we could do about it except to pull the boat out of the lock to a suitable mooring. Naturally, by a deep lock on a river (we were now on the River Soar) there is a large weir and we found it extremely difficult to control the boat merely by holding the ropes.

Finally we tied up about 400 yards past the lock. It was now five o'clock and dark and both of us looked forward to a hot meal and bed. I, for once, gave myself the luxury of a hot water bottle, something rare indeed, as although I like a warm bed, I usually leave it too late for the bottle to warm it up in time. But tonight, I put one in the bed before dinner. By eight o'clock we were both sleepy and I jumped eagerly into my warm, cosy bed to find it was not only warm but wet ... the bottle had leaked.

It took nearly an hour to dry the mattress and remake the bed with fresh sheets. Then I fell asleep, hoping that a launderette wasn't too far away as I now had wet sweaters, thick woollen socks, sheets, pillowcases ...

Kegworth did indeed have a launderette and although I had never before washed sweaters in a machine, the lady in charge told me everything would be all right ... use cool water and a cool dryer she said, and I did. Kegworth was obviously not my kind of town, for now I have three thick-knits which will fit two of my grandchildren perfectly. I'm rather glad that once the cable is mended we shall have only one more day on the River Soar. I don't think it likes canal boats using it.

11

From the end of the River Soar, we found ourselves faced with a choice of navigation. Either we could take the Cranfleet Cut, or the Erewash Canal, or go along the River Trent itself until we met up with Trent lock and entered the Trent and Mersey Canal. Deciding on the latter we turned into the River Trent where we immediately felt the force of its strong contrary current. We seemed barely to move and as we watched the trees alongside us, we saw indeed that we were having a struggle to hold our own. Owen remembered then that the current was weakest nearer the shore, so we edged in close and made a little progress, but only just.

The Trent lock ahead looked rather large and I hoped that we could manage it between us. As we neared, the gates opened. To our surprise – and relief – we found a lock-keeper in charge. Indeed this lock is always manned. We gratefully accepted his help with the lock-work especially as fog began to form; by the time we left the lock, visibility was poor indeed. Although we knew the chances were minimal we decided to stop early in case we met a working boat.

The next day we visited Shardlow, a much written-about canal centre. In the old days, a great deal of traffic used this part of the canal but sad to say, only a few of the original canal side warehouses and offices still stand. However, it has the air of a pretty little backwater and still has an appeal for the boater who is looking for peace and quiet.

The fog surrounded us for the next day or two and we made little progress. At Burton-on-Trent, I was due to broadcast on Radio Derby, but I had lost my voice and had developed a heavy catarrhal cold, so Owen went instead and found himself taking part in a morning chat programme alongside the local Women's Institute members. It came off very well, I thought, as I lay in bed hugging a hot water bottle and listening on my transistor.

The editor of *Waterways World*, Bob Shopland, paid us a visit while we were moored at Burton. He took the boat for a short run and thought she handled very well indeed. He also took photos of Owen and *Bix*, but I was still too choked up with my cold to take part in any of the day's outing ... I just lay in bed while the boat chugged up and down the canal.

By the time we reached the village of Alrewas, I was better. Two days in bed with lots of hot lemon and honey had done the trick, and although it was still foggy, I thought a walk around this pretty black and white village would do me good. In any case, we had to call in at the post office to collect our mail. The lady clerk seemed flustered as Owen asked if there was any post for us. She hastily whispered to someone hidden behind the partition, 'it's the man for that packet.' We smiled at what was obviously an unusual occurrence for Alrewas post office. The lady produced a large envelope of letters and said, 'that's 10p please.' Owen explained that there was no charge; it was not a poste-restante address, just a packet posted to the post office to be collected. But she insisted on making her charge.

As we didn't think it worthwhile making a fuss over 10p we paid up, explaining that we collected our mail weekly in this manner all over England and this was the first time we had been asked for money. As the money and packet changed hands, she smiled and said, 'you see it costs us money not to deliver it to you.' That stumped us. We left speechless.

Later that day, we reached Fradley Junction, where the Coventry Canal meets the Trent and Mersey Canal. A convenient telephone kiosk by the side of the canal bridge allowed us to ring our second daughter Marny, or to be more correct her husband Keith, when we heard the splendid news that their son Benjamin had been born earlier that day.

While dinner was cooking, we went into the Swan to celebrate grandchild number four. As we sat before a roaring coal fire, the bar to ourselves, I wondered just when I would see Marny and her baby and for an instant I regretted not being nearer to the family. A friendly greeting from someone entering the bar brought me out of my reverie: it was an employee of the BWB whom we'd seen earlier while going through the locks outside Alrewas.

'Glad to see you again,' he said. 'Tell me did you call your boat *Bix* after Beiderbecke?' And that's how we met Terry McNally from Colwich lock, his wife Val and their two children. He joined us in a drink to celebrate Benjamin's arrival and before he left we'd covered a variety of subjects, with music being foremost amongst them. He gave us strict instructions about always knocking on his door when going through Colwich lock; there would always be a cup of tea for us ... needless to say, we have done so on many occasions, finishing up one session at two in the morning, enjoying home made wine as we played solo whist!

Next morning we started travelling along the Coventry Canal, once again the countryside opening out in wide vistas on either side. After a while, we noticed that the bridge numbering seemed inconsistent. Later we learned that this end of the Coventry Canal had been started by the Birmingham Fazeley Canal Company, a smaller canal which joins the Coventry Canal. The Birmingham and Fazeley ran out of money and the Coventry Canal Company completed it with the result that we now have mixed bridge architecture as well as jumbled numbers.

The Coventry Canal offers varied scenery; open country followed by the back gardens of a new housing estate. Then, farmland again, a deep woodland cutting, an isolated canal cottage which looks so pretty from the canal side until you notice that the railway company have built a level crossing almost on its front doorstep.

We moored at Tamworth, well, Glascote really. Tamworth proper is about a mile from the canal. The locks approaching Glascote are flanked by factories and steel works, but surprisingly, once past the locks there is a pub, handy for mooring, then it's open country again.

We walked into Tamworth to shop and explore. The Castle is well worth studying, especially the beautiful herring-bone brickwork on its walls. A path leads up and up the outside of the castle until you reach the top from where a panoramic view of Tamworth and the surrounding country rewards you.

I began to realise that I was missing the services of a regular hairdresser, something that had not occurred to me when buying the boat. I wear my hair in a straight short style that calls for expert cutting and I had used the same hairdresser for years. On the two occasions my hair was cut during the previous few months, I had felt very much the odd-woman out. If Madam hasn't got a regular assistant who does her hair, then Madam is given some very odd looks indeed.

After Tamworth, the next stop was Atherstone where I saw for the first time a shop that not only advertised cutting as a speciality but blow waving as well. Immediately I went in to make an appointment. A large young man with blue hair hardly took his eyes off the rollers he was releasing from a newly permed head. Would 3 o'clock do? I replied yes and he gave me a quick smile and said OK.

As I left the shop, I told myself to be prepared for a long wait as he hadn't bothered to consult his appointments book or even make a note of my time. I duly arrived just before three. There were two wash-basins for shampooing at one side of the room, two setting tables in the centre and a door leading off into the back of the shop.

An enormous mirror in a mahogany frame, about four feet by five feet was leaning against another wall, partly covering an opening through which I could see a flight of stairs leading above the shop.

My blue haired young man was busy with a client while a young girl with bright orange hair with mauve streaks in it was shampooing, removing rollers, getting clients seated and ready for trims and sets, and darting about between the five or six clients who somehow or other were all being attended to by this incredible staff of two.

I wondered where to put my coat. There were no hooks or hangers anywhere – and no spare chairs.

'Hang it over the mirror love,' said Blue Hair.

'I suppose you'll get it fixed one day,' said a client, pointing to the mirror.

'It's too big, anyway,' said Orange Hair from the basin end.

The argument about the mirror and when it would be fixed was interrupted by an elderly woman putting her head round the door.

'Can I come in about a quarter to six tonight?' Blue Hair paused for a second before replying, 'Yes, but be pronto. Ta love, see you.'

I found myself being expertly shampooed, seated at the table and waiting, but not for long. I explained my usual style and the scissors started straight away. My usual reticence in a new hairdressers dissolved in the family-kitchen atmosphere. Conversation bounced from wall to wall as client chatted to client, staff to client, staff to staff. ...

51

A woman entered and walked through the shop into the back room. Five minutes later, she popped her head in to ask Blue Hair, 'how many?' He counted heads, asked me if I took sugar, obviously knowing everyone else's tastes, and a few minutes later a tray of tea appeared. Some customers were on their second cup when two schoolgirls entered. 'Hallo,' they greeted us and then chattered to Blue Hair about their day at school, their boyfriends, the disco they were visiting later that night. Meanwhile my hair was being expertly cut and blow dried, and people were still asking, usually from the doorway, if they could be washed, permed, coloured, but on Monday, Tuesday 3 o'clock, 2 o'clock. Without once consulting a book, Blue Hair said yes, no, make it half an hour later, or earlier.

Young Blue Hair, in fact, was everyone's blue-eyed boy. From the conversation most of them had known him since he was a schoolboy, the older women acting like his mum. 'I suppose you have eaten something today?'

The dryers were upstairs and most of the clients went up and seated themselves under them. When one elderly lady was asked if she wanted help, she threatened to tan Blue Hair's backside with his own hairbrush. But I noticed he popped upstairs a few minutes afterwards to check.

I had no idea how much the cost of my afternoon would be as I could see no price list, but I'd had such a marvellous time and my hair looked and felt so good, that I knew I wouldn't begrudge it if the cost was more than I normally paid. Blue Hair said that he too was pleased with the result and hoped I would come again when in the area. I assured him I would and then he presented the bill: 50p. I couldn't believe it but he assured me that was his charge for shampoo, cut and blow wave. No, no charge for the cup of tea. What a splendid character to meet and in all places a ladies hairdressers.

I rang my daughter Linda, the usual weekly call to let her know where to redirect the post. Before I could tell about my unusual afternoon, she silenced me by saying, 'There's a Mr Clive Jacobs, a BBC reporter looking for you. Ring him and tell him exactly where you are. He wants to do a programme about you and dad for You and Yours, and oh yes,' she went on, 'ring the Woman's Hour producer, she wants you as well.'

Well, I thought as I clambered back on board, what a good job I had my hair done after all.

12

The last half of the Coventry Canal, from Atherstone on to Coventry itself can be pretty depressing. The villages of Mancetter and Hartshill are given over almost entirely to quarrying, although Hartshill does have a redeeming factor in the lovely old buildings restored and used by the BWB at their boat yard tucked beneath the mountainous slag heaps. One building has a graceful clock tower atop its roof and long ago this must have been a proud etching against the sky. Alas, no longer, as the slag heaps have overtaken it.

The canal water is heavily polluted on this stretch, and a dredger is in constant use to combat the waste forever pouring in from leaky pipes, broken gutters, and other appliances connected with the quarrying. To cruise along this stretch is for all the world as if you are sailing through gallons of tomato soup.

At Nuneaton, the waters clear a little and then, within a mile or so of the Coventry Basin, become so pure that you can see the plants growing from the bottom — and the prams, bikes and mattresses as well.

Nuneaton or to be exact Arbury, a mile outside the town, is George Eliot's birthplace. We walked around the George Eliot rooms which are set aside in the local museum, but none of its exhibits moved me, telling little or nothing about the authoress. Since I was 10 years old, when I won *The Mill on the Floss* as a school prize I have wanted to know more about this writer. I failed to finish the book, finding it too difficult at that age and losing it during the war. I have yet to read anything by George Eliot and the museum didn't encourage me to try.

Our journey took us further up the canal past the unnavigable Griff Arm which was built to carry coal from the Griff Colliery, but is now overgrown and derelict. We moored and walked along this once thriving part of the canal system, the tall trees on both sides of the canal almost meeting overhead to form a green tunnel. Beneath this seeming tropical canopy the birds sang with more vigour, their songs trilling from end to end of the enchanted place. Then a dramatic change of scenery: the trees ended abruptly to reveal the sky. We climbed the steep sides of the cutting and found ourselves on what might have been the surface of the moon.

Huge craters opened before and around us, the rest of the landscape comprising broad deserts of red soil. In some craters a greenish water swirled, the very places described by George Eliot as the Red Deeps in her book *Mill on the Floss*. At last I began to find an interest in the lady. We were so impressed that we stayed the night, and next day visited Arbury Hall on whose estate George Eliot's father had been a farm bailiff. As a girl she had visited the Hall often when her father went to report on the day's business.

Arbury Hall is two miles walk from the canal, but well worth the visit, if only to see the tapestry chair covers, sewn by the mistress of the house sometime in the early 19th century. This particular lady asked her husband's advice on what design she should use for new chair covers. As she was so untidy, he said, and always left her hat, gloves, scarves and handkerchiefs lying on the chairs why not incorporate them in the design. Which is precisely what she did – today when you walk into the room at Arbury Hall you really believe that someone has left a scarf trailing over the seat, or a glove has been pushed to the back of the cushion. Only when you seek to pick them up do you realise that they are part of the tapestry design itself.

The next day we decided to go to Coventry, passing by the junction of the Ashby Canal, to leave the Ashby for another time.

We were soon travelling through the heart of industrial Coventry where we passed a huge chemical factory that seemed to stretch for miles and smelling strongly of vinegar. The canal has a couple of sharp bends to navigate before reaching Coventry basin in the heart of the city itself. The mooring could not have been better. Imagine tying up your home just five minutes walk from the Cathedral and shops.

I looked forward to exploring Coventry. In fact, we had visited the Cathedral two years earlier on a motoring trip, on the spur of the moment deciding to lunch in Coventry. But driving is the worst of all ways to explore any city these days, now we could take our time and walk.

To date, I fear, I had visited no large town or city in the midlands or north of England. And now, in the space of a few months, I could find my way around the shopping centres of Leicester, Loughborough, Birmingham, Derby and, of course, Coventry.

Each had something to offer, not only local foods but different systems – like the supermarket that has its check-out tills back to front. Your basket is placed in front of the girl at her till. She removes the items, rings them up, then returns them to the conveyor belt which takes them away from where you are standing. If you don't have anyone at the other end, they either fall off or all pile up on top of one another.

In Coventry, it was the wool shop that fascinated me. I had decided to knit a sweater for my new grandson and walked around looking for the wool I required. The walls were stocked from top to bottom, an assistant filling empty spaces. I found a gorgeous dark olive green; alas, only one ball on the shelf. A deep chestnut and dark brown tweedie mixture suggested it would make a good substitute; again a single ball only.

By this time, Owen was getting fed up with our shopping spree and suggested I should ask if they had any more of the colour I wanted in their stock room.

At the cash desk the girl took the balls of green and chestnut, and asked how much I required. To my next question, she replied I could have either colour. I gave my order for the green whereupon she threw both balls into a wire basket, and spoke through a walkie-talkie fixed to the wall behind her. A few moments later, a bag containing my wool slid down a chute from the stock-room. I peeped inside the bag and sure enough there was my green wool. As I paid the assistant explained. The shop contained one ball of every type and colour stocked. Upstairs they kept the rest of the stock to be sold to the customers below. It reduced handling. The wire basket was emptied regularly to replace the balls selected by customers, these much handled wools being sold off cheaply throughout the year. I wondered why other wool shops haven't copied them.

By now Easter was upon us when we were looking forward to having our first visitors to stay on board. It would be a challenge to see if we could cope with entertaining and cooking for four days for three extra people. Our daughter, Linda, her husband Ian and their son, two year old Lewis had decided to spend Easter with us.

We thought we would cruise the Ashby Canal so said a regretful farewell to Coventry and retraced our journey down to the Ashby. I felt the first mild rays of the Spring sunshine and got quite excited at the thought of how I'd show off our new home, and how Lewis would love to see the moorhens nesting ...

It was grand seeing some of our family again. The boat accommodated us all without our feeling we were living on top of each other. Linda and Ian took our bedroom while we slept on the bed settee. Lewis slept on the music room floor, wrapped up in a sleeping bag on a nest of cushions. He loved his 'special bed.'

The meals were no problem. I had given dinner parties aboard and could cope easily with the catering. If only the weather had been more spring-like ... Easter, 1975, must have broken all records for snow, frost, ice, sleet and bitter, bitter cold winds.

We had about two hours of watery sunshine on Easter Monday when the sky blackened and a blizzard swept the countryside. Thus it was that Lewis saw no moorhens and Linda saw little of the canal scenery. Even the day they left was a miserable one, a freezing fog soon swallowing their car as they sped back to London. But we had enjoyed being together again and the Summer lay before us for more trips together.

After they had gone, we cruised the whole canal again, all 21 miles of it – with no locks. It really is a lovely canal, rural countryside throughout its whole length. Its only drawback is its shallowness. We could moor only in two places, (apart from a water-point and the one and only boat yard at Stoke Golding near which there is a colony of yellow wagtails). Never before have I seen so many of these shy birds. The pied and the grey wagtails are fairly common, but so often have I spotted a yellow one only to find on closer inspection that it was really a grey.

We also had a chance to walk back through history: the canal runs alongside the fields where the Battle of Bosworth was fought in 1485. The day we trudged through them, it was easy to understand why so many men and their horses floundered in the mire. For most of the way it was marshland and we grew colder and colder as we squelched towards our goal, a small museum at the back of a farm where Leicester County Council have exhibits and models showing the plan of campaign. We discovered that we had moored our boat at the bottom of the field where legend has it that Henry Tudor picked up Richard's crown and was himself crowned King of England. To this day that field is called Crown Hill.

As we chugged along the last stretch of the Ashby — a bird's paradise — we were accompanied by dozens and dozens of robins, singing and piping jauntily; every bough seemed to have a bird flaunting his colourful feathers to greet the spring sunshine which belatedly had decided to make an appearance. If only Lewis were with us now! But life never turns out quite perfect, does it?

13

Spring was well and truly here: tiny spearheads uncurled on the hawthorn bushes, the grass grew a richer green and the sun shone every day. Not very warm, but at least everything sparkled in this brighter world around us.

We continued down the Coventry, this time to join the Oxford Canal at Hawkesbury Junction, another well-known canal centre where history surrounds you not only in the shape of the old ruined pumping house, the still very much alive canal pub and cottages, but also in the form of Joe and Rosie Skinner.

Here Mr and Mrs Skinner live on board their boat *Friendship*, the last two people to operate a transport company on the canals, the last of the real working boat people. Anyone who has read some history of the canals must have heard of *Friendship* and her owners. We felt proud indeed when, on passing them for the third time, Rosie came out to have a chat. When I told her we were hoping to do some shopping before going down the Oxford, she recommended Bedworth as it had a market the following day where I could pick up good, cheap vegetables.

Bedworth was once a mining town, and before that, Flemish ribbon weavers settled there. Today, the tradition of ribbon weaving is still carried on under a name that is famous throughout the world. Cash's name ribbons are made here and the houses that the weavers lived in still stand, although somewhat depleted after the heavy bombing raids on Coventry. Cash's Buildings, as they are known, feature in many a holiday maker's photographs, as they stand by the side of the canal, their glorious deep mellowed red brick facades adding a splash of colour to this somewhat dreary stretch of industrial canal.

Bedworth we found rather dull and although I did manage to buy some cheap vegetables and cheap hanks of knitting wool, direct from the mills, once we'd finished shopping we were eager to return to our floating home. A cup of coffee would have proved acceptable but we couldn't find a decent morning coffee shop in the town. I like my morning coffee taken in a restful, comfortable place, not one with blaring juke boxes and all chrome and 'help yourself', all that we could find in Bedworth.

Our luck changed when Owen noticed the blackboard propped up against one side of a gateway. Morning coffee, it said, and an arrow directed us through the gateway. We found ourselves transported back a century or two, standing in a courtyard flanked by quaint terraced houses, with galleried apartments upstairs.

Another notice pinned on to a door told us to enter, so in we went and found ourselves in a room reminiscent of a Woman's Institute committee meeting, except that the ladies sitting around small tables were drinking coffee, instead of listening to Madam President.

Someone came forward and welcomed us warmly. Owen, as the only male in the room, was eyed curiously. We were directed to a table, asked how we liked our coffee, and when it arrived it was accompanied by a generous plateful of biscuits ... the price 10p! Our waitress, seeing our interest in the unusual venue, explained that we were in the almshouses and the ladies of the local church organised this weekly coffee morning to aid the funds.

The buildings were indeed attractive and when I asked how old they were, our waitress asked if we would like to go on an inspection. Would we? Knowing my avid curiousity about everything and anything, especially social history, Owen gave up all ideas of moving the boat any further that day. And so we spent a delightful hour walking around the houses and gardens and hearing some of the stories about their background.

The almshouses were built in 1840 by a Mr Chamberlayne and they not only provided housing for the old and the poor, but beauty too. A lovely entrance hall, complete with minstrel's gallery and warm panelled rooms surrounding the hall. When I saw a bookcase containing the parish diaries of the past vicars, my appetite was further whetted. I wondered what was inside those stiff covers? Our guide asked if I'd like to read through them. She could easily get the key of the bookcase for me and she was sure that it wouldn't matter if I stayed for the rest of the day. But a firm refusal from Owen made me shake my head. As much as I would have loved to have read through them, I couldn't really expect him to stand around waiting for the next couple of hours or so. Anyway, I could always keep this treat as something special to do when I found myself in this area again.

From Hawkesbury Junction, we sailed beneath the lovely old iron bridge which carries the towpath across the junction of the two canals. We were now back on the Oxford Canal again, a favourite of mine. Last seen during the winter, we now looked at familiar scenery with different eyes. In spring towpath and hedgerow are bursting with wild flowers and as we travelled peacefully along, we spent many hours watching mallards, swans, and moorhens busy at their nest-making.

Moorhens are extremely fussy about this. Obviously the females know just how they want the nest built. The male spends most of his time swimming beneath overhanging branches in search of pieces of reed, grass, even thin whispy twigs, only to find in some cases that his ladylove doesn't like what he has to offer. He watches disconsolately as she throws them back in the water.

Near Brinklow, we watched a male moorhen swimming valiantly for quite a distance, a long leaf from an underwater plant had been laboriously tugged out and now straddled across his face like a huge moustache, its ends trailing in the water making two more wakes at his side. Madam was treading down grasses and waving bits of reed mace round and round the nest, precariously balanced on the low branches of a hazel tree. It was also near a bridge, a silly place I thought to build a nest. At last, an exhausted male finally arrived and passed over his extra large offering. It took her less than a second to look at it, pick it up and chuck it back at him. She then continued to weave *her* material in and out, building up the sides of a circular, well-padded home.

We had already seen the first of the hire boats and each day brought more. I worried whether a beginner to steering would be able to avoid hitting the moorhen's nest, but to my astonishment, when we finally tore ourselves away and had to pass it, we found that we missed it entirely by the time we had got the boat in line to pass under the bridge. We watched a hirer going through the other way and the same thing happened. By the time he was through and had straightened up, the nest was some yards off. I wonder if the moorhen knew she had chosen a safe spot. Since then, we have seen hundreds of them, so many looking as if the wash from the boats, would capsize them but this never seems to happen.

We moored one night by the side of a small glade called All Oaks Wood and although a road ran along the edge of the trees, we were surrounded by squirrels, wagtails and a noisy blackbird busily sounding his warning song as well he might; there was a kestrel overhead. We could hear but not see a woodpecker drilling away but were compensated by the sight of a stoat strolling casually along the canal bank at dusk. I thought how lucky we were to have such a lovely 'wallpaper' around us, but the next morning Owen had second thoughts as the dawn chorus started up no more than three feet from our bed. After Owen had asked what time it was, twice in about three minutes, I decided to stop oohing and aahing and trying to recognise the different bird calls.

Next night in contrast we tied up ten yards from a bus stop ... we were in Rugby.

In most books the canal scene is described as tranquil, peaceful, a rural back-door to England, but we were finding out that there was also an other side, where the grass, if you can find any, certainly isn't greener. Of course, the canals were built as a transport system to carry coke, clay and lime from pit to factory and the finished product from factory to depot. But, nowadays, the rural country canal degenerates swiftly into urban development; huge council estates, rubbish tips, and, of course, motorways. It's a peculiar sensation to cruise at two miles per hour alongside the M1 for instance. As a one-time car driver, averaging 700 miles a week for many years, I now found it incredible that I had once sat behind a steering wheel behaving, from a boatman's view, like a lunatic.

At Rugby, we moored alongside a new housing development and although the road was but a few yards from our door, there was as yet little traffic. We were thankful for this relatively quiet spot a day or so later when we added what is to date the most interesting and beautiful photo to our collection.

Seated outside eating our lunch we heard a commotion behind the boat. Three swans swam up and down, two male and one female. The chosen cob was clearly telling the other he was now in the way and would he kindly shove off which eventually he did. The cob and pen swam one way and the rejected suitor the other. But after a few yards he decided to return and try again.

The two male birds hissed, swam round and round, aiming blows at each other with beaks, necks and wings until, victory regained, our pair swam off and the loser slowly swam away down current.

As I cleared the plates I noticed that yet another attempt was to be made, this time the victor deciding to speed up the other's departure. They swam furiously towards each other and fought again. This time our rejected suitor took the hint and fled. To be sure he had gone for good, the other cob took flight also their wings clattering as they became airborne. The first flew fast but the second swan gained on him until by stretching out his long long neck, while still flying, he could give a sharp nip to his rival's backside. We have a fantastic shot of the very moment when that vicious snap of the beak descended. This was the end — our pair of swans swam off to their end of the canal while lonely heart kept his distance at the other. He swam back and forth under the bridge and was there the next day, but made no more attempts to join the others. He could have been a rival male or perhaps one of their own offspring grown up enough to leave home, but a bit slow on the uptake and dad had to show him that he meant it.

When the films were developed, I was thrilled. I'd taken the colour transparencies and Owen the cine, and both were excellent. I'm far from being an expert with the camera, but at last I have something to compensate for all the film I've wasted on herons. Owen says I must have the biggest collection of non-heron pictures in the world. I'll never understand why it is that herons stand still for ages in a perfect pose until I lift the camera to my eye and click ... they've flown away. I've hidden in the front well of the boat; laid flat on the roof; sat for hours on the towpath: but all I have to show for my patience are endless backgrounds — heronless.

We had neighbours at Rugby: a young married couple living with their two-year-old son in an unfinished narrow boat. With another baby on the way, they must have been extremely resilient to survive the primitive conditions they had been reduced to. With no water tank on board, they had to be even more careful than we were as they used it from a ten gallon container. They had one gas fire only and the bed and kitchen shelves were the only other fittings. A table and stools completed their furnishing but they were deliriously happy the day we arrived because, at long last, they had got a completion date on a canal-side cottage they were buying. In fact, that afternoon, they had obtained the key and the following day they were going to move the boat down the canal, about a mile, to Clifton, where they would be able to moor it at the bottom of their own garden.

The next day, they came on board for a coffee and to say goodbye and after this we stood on deck to wave to them. We wondered why Dave was still on the towpath holding the ropes, when to our astonishment, he started to walk, pulling the boat behind him.

The boat had no engine: he was prepared to pull it and his family to their cottage. Owen jumped on to the towpath and ran after him and, of course, within a few minutes we had started up our engine and were in front of them, passing over the tow. How grand to see two young people prepared to work and go without, to achieve their goal.

One of a Victorian terrace built for canal folk the cottage stood in the middle, with two small rooms downstairs, two upstairs and an outdoor lavatory. A long narrow garden ran down to the canal, and in the centre of it stood a lovely old plum tree.

They took us over their new home, telling us of their plans for redecorating, about the extension Dave had designed. We, in turn, gave them advice on clearing up the garden and before we left, it had been decided that we should have dinner with them that very night. They insisted, it was their 'thank you' for the tow. So we moored at the bottom of their garden and during the afternoon we wandered around Rugby, but we were shocked by the high cost of bus fares there and walked back to the boat which gave us quite an appetite for dinner. As we washed and dressed, we heard a knock on the door. It was our hostess asking if we could eat the meal in our boat as ours was so much nicer than theirs. So we sat down to dinner in our own home, but cooked by our friend from the boat next door!

14

At Braunston Turn, we joined the Grand Union and the southern part of the Oxford Canal. It had been winter when we last travelled along these waters – now the branches of the trees were bursting into leaf, making dancing reflections in the canal.

Although bound for Oxford, we decided to turn into the Grand Union and moor again at Braunston, such a convenient village to stock up on groceries and it had a launderette.

As we approached the junction of the canals, I went to the front of the boat to start our usual mooring routine ... by now so well worked out that we needed few if any words or signs between captain and crew. My drill was to get out the two mooring spikes and mallet, then, with the front rope ready in my hand, prepare to jump off with it from the front of the boat.

As I went forward to the front well, I thought how much easier it all was when travelling on waters we knew, when one could tell exactly what the mooring would be like ... how wide the towpath was ... how near we could get the boat into the side. So I find it difficult to put into words my shock when on turning into the Grand Union I saw, moored where we were heading for, a submarine! It was impossible to shout to Owen, 65 feet is a long length of narrow boat to get round a sharp bend and he had yet to see what lay ahead. I ran back through the boat and shouted to him, 'there's a submarine tied up, we can't get in.'

His eyes widened. 'A what?'

He gave me a strange look then, 'Christ!'

By now we were past the junction and approaching the mooring, and there they were, outside the Rose and Castle pub, a destroyer and a submarine. As we came alongside, we were given a wave by the captain and some of Her Majesty's sailors. We tied up opposite to them and two of their crew came over and all was explained. The submarine and destroyer were part of a recruiting campaign for the Royal Navy, an annual occurrence when they travelled the canals and river in their models scaled down for inland waters. Both vessels, of course, were open to the public.

While our neighbours busied themselves getting the craft shipshape, we took a break in the pub for a refreshing lager before lunch. It was nice to be greeted as old friends by the staff, but I think it was the boat they remembered more than us. We were beginning to get known by quite a lot of people, especially since the hire boats had started.

Two American ladies, having lunch by the windows overlooking the canal, stared down on to *Bix*. Realising that we were the owners, they started asking questions about our boat and the canals. When they found out that we actually lived on *Bix* permanently, one of them went outside on to the verandah. She returned to ask again if we actually meant that *Bix* was in place of a home. We assured her that it was our only home and we had lived on board now for almost seven months. She just shook her head 'My, my – it's like living in a banana!' We drank up and went off to our own lunch ... that is after unzipping the banana, of course.

I felt quite ruffled by such a description of our home so after shopping I had a quiet sit down to recover in Braunston church, with its lovely old watering can by the font, painted in the traditional canal style. I also met up again with the local baker who remembered me and gave a nod. It was nice to feel some sense of belonging ... this travelling life of ours does give one a feeling of living on the fringe of the world, of not actually belonging anywhere. We have no regular postman, no milkman, no dustman, no real neighbours, but we were building up a steady stream of acquaintances as we moved along the canals.

As I walked across the footpath leading down the hill to the canal, I could see Owen in the back of the boat, talking to a man on the other side of the canal. As I approached the boat, I saw to my astonishment that it was the well-known canal character, Arthur Bray, the last of the Number Ones to continue boating. He retired in 1970, and now lives aboard his boat which is moored at Braunston. Much has been written about the history of the canals and especially the Number Ones, the owner-boatmen who worked on the canals, and in Arthur Bray, we have a slice of living history.

But with the tremendous surge of interest in canals making hundreds of enthusiasts flock by boat or car to them throughout the year, Arthur has found his retirement less peaceful than expected. Unconsciously, because like most waterways folk he is a quiet, retiring man, he stays shut up in his boat whenever strangers are near, not because he doesn't like people, but today's crowds seem alien to his idea of the canals. But now that he had seen *Bix* on three or four occasions, he had come along to find out a bit more about us and I hope we get to know more about him as well. I felt another little glow inside me as I waved goodbye to Arthur, at least someone made us feel as if we belonged to the canals ... banana indeed!

We retraced our journey through Napton, Cropredy and Banbury, this time sharing the work of the lift bridges with other holiday-makers on the boats, and then we continued on to Oxford.

We passed by beautiful woods and I fell in love with so many pretty houses and cottages. For the first time, we had to wait our turn at locks while other boats went through; the hire season was now in full swing. We began to see the same boats week after week and soon got to know the different boatyards' colours and names. 'Here comes Buttonweed again,' and we'd wave gaily at the holiday-makers who must have often wondered why we were so pleased to see them, not realising it was the boat we were greeting.

On one occasion, we moored near a well-known-to-us boat and made friends with the hirer. When we told him that we often saw his boat, he invited us to look inside. And, of course, afterwards we entertained this schoolmaster from Bedales with his wife and family on board *Bix*. Like all who came aboard, they were surprised to see such a luxurious, comfortable home. The piano, of course is always greeted with amazement. The 30 foot lounge which has no fitted furniture, furnished with my farm's dining room pieces, coffee table, settee, hi-fi and a small corner TV, plus my favourite pictures hanging on the end bulkhead, seem to raise envy amongst the female visitors. All that space and so little housework!

Owen decided to pay his mother another visit in hospital when we reached Lower Heyford. The railway ran alongside the canal here and the station was only a few yards from the towpath, convenient for travelling but noisy for mooring. The next morning, I sat up in bed and waved to Owen as he sat in his corner railway seat, about 20 yards from the boat.

Lower Heyford itself is such a pretty village. Just like a picture postcard where visiting Americans could certainly stand and stare, if only their wretched aeroplanes didn't make so much noise. An American air base is situated on the outskirts of the village and so constant are their flying exercises that a whole section of the canal is marked off as not fit to moor overnight, due to excess noise from aircraft.

Soon, we were on the outskirts of Oxford and back to lift bridges again. Owen was struggling with one when a cyclist came along the towpath. He rode over the bridge, threw down his bike and helped to heave the bridge open. As I steered underneath it, I saw that our helper was the man we had met during the winter when he had been pulling his boat to Oxford. What a coincidence to meet again and yet even as I write those words, I know it's not. We were so often to meet up again with what we had thought of as 'ships passing in the night'.

Our friend told us that we would soon be passing his boat, which he was still painting, on a nearby temporary mooring. He had been out of work all winter. Each day he had cycled in and around Oxford looking for work but had found nothing. He asked our advice, but we really couldn't help not knowing the area at all. He hoped we would find Oxford a happier place than he had.

In fact we had a very pleasant stay in Oxford. We phoned two friends who lived in Abingdon and arranged to have dinner with them but before this we invited them for drinks aboard.

Like most people who live in a town or village that has a canal, our friends were ignorant of just where the canal was in Oxford ... the river they knew of course but the canal?

When told we were tied up almost outside Worcester College, near Hythe Gate Street bridge, Jackie's comment was, 'wow, what an address.'

It was a superb mooring, so near to the city centre and yet so quiet that a pair of swans were foolishly making a nest on the towpath. A local inhabitant informed us that it was a yearly event, but unfortunately, no eggs ever hatched as the local youths stole them. I find it hard to believe that no one has done anything to protect these birds at mating time. If town won't, why not gown?

Although this was our first visit to Oxford by canal, we were no

A convenient mooring for Coventry cathedral and shops (five minutes away)

Pinching out tomato shoots — they will soon reach the roof

Kibworth Lock — Leicester section

Five minutes from Paddington Station (Regents Canal)

The Shovel Inn canal pub at Cowley, Grand Union canal

strangers to the city and I remembered to stock up on coffee beans from the little coffee blenders tucked away in the market place.

As much as we would have loved to stay in Oxford, we decided it was time to move off once again and so two days later, we said goodbye and made our way back to Coventry.

The return journey down the Oxford canal was every bit as delightful as the outward one. You discover so many new things when travelling in the opposite direction: Flights Mill, for instance, a lovely house dating back to 1204, near Pigeons Lock. This looks so attractive when coming from Oxford, the lovely dark tunnel of the approaching woods making a perfect backdrop to the beautiful old stone walls.

We had an easy journey back through Braunston, Rugby, and in no time at all we were at Coventry. Another change in the scenery for us, for the untidy, depressing backs of the factories were now partially hidden by graceful, fully leaved branches from the poor trees struggling to survive in the muck and debris floating around their roots.

There was clear water in Coventry and I must say again that the lovely old canal basin with its toll house, now put to good use by the local canal society, makes a warm and welcoming greeting to boats visiting the city.

15

Summer is a-cumin in ... and bringing with it many welcome visitors, our son, daughters, sons-in-law, grandchildren, friends, old neighbours from Kent. The summer weeks went by swiftly, each day the weathermen telling us that all records were being broken. Our visitors exclaimed how lucky we were to live this happy, carefree life, and we agreed.

We took them back along the Coventry, showing off our newly found knowledge of boating, buildings, and the various places and people we passed. And then it was new, uncharted waters for us.

We turned off the Coventry canal along the Birmingham and Fazely, and discovered again just how closely the rural countryside creeps up to the edge of our large towns and cities.

The Birmingham and Fazely is a small junction canal linking the Coventry canal with the main line Birmingham canal system. We joined it at Fazeley Junction and travelled through Drayton Bassett, passing Drayton Manor, once the home of Sir Robert Peel, and now a park and zoo. Much of the landscape of this canal is bleak, the open fields occasionally broken by a sparsely wooded copse.

At Bodymore Heath, we awaited the arrival of our two folding bikes. We had experienced a slight snag when it came to ordering by mail order. Where could they be sent? It was no use having them delivered to our daughter's address as for our letters. She couldn't get them to us. Then we thought of Terry, our BWB friend from Colwich lock. We sent off our order giving his address for delivery, then we telephoned him and told him. In due course another call to him, and he gave us the news that the bikes had arrived and he would bring them over when he visited his in-laws in Birmingham. We had a happy re-union when he brought them along one Saturday afternoon, seemingly every bit as excited about the bikes as we were.

The next morning, Owen and I decided to have a trial run. Bodymore Heath is a hamlet consisting of a few houses, a pub and a farm. The land around looks pretty flat so we set off for a pleasant morning's cycle ride down the lane and along the next road where, almost immediately the flat land gave way to a long, long hill. After this we had a stretch of main road in front of us before turning back on a quieter minor road to the boat. The whole journey was about six miles and how my leg muscles were rebelling. I hadn't cycled since 1943 and found the difference in traffic quite frightening. How close those huge juggernauts came and what a strong draught of wind they made, almost taking me off the bike. I hoped that my future rides would be on minor roads wherever possible.

66

We had already discussed where to keep the machines; you haven't much of a choice really with a home like ours. Many boat-owners keep them on the roof of the boat, but as we prefer to keep *Bix* looking neat and trim, they had to go inside the boat. But where? We measured the bikes and walked up and down the lounge, bedroom, music room, galley and ... suddenly we found it. Now if they both fitted it was the perfect place. They did, just, and so now we keep our bikes ... well, it's a secret. You have to come on board and look for them yourselves. It makes a lovely conversation opener when visitors are with us!

A few miles on from Bodymore Heath industry takes over again, but for once, at Tyburn, a factory had appreciated its position on the canal. The Cincinatti Company have landscaped the side of the canal that runs by their factory, and very eye-catching yet simple it is too, with sloping banks covered with beautifully kept grass and low-spreading shrubs. It cheered us up to see at last an industrial concern interested in the canal.

Small steel works, tower blocks of factories, the big Dunlop square-blocked factory with its flag a-flying, we steered past all these and on to Salford Junction where we slowly moved between huge concrete pillars, looking for the canal to take us towards Bordsley. We had a choice of the Tame Valley Canal, continuing along the Birmingham and Fazeley or taking the short junction towards Bordsley.

These canals meeting at Salford Junction gave us a good idea of just how much traffic had used this part of the canal system in days gone by. It wasn't hard to imagine the stream of boats turning off into one or other of them; there had probably been traffic jams in those days, too.

It must have reflected the scene above for the concrete pillars we passed between carried Spaghetti Junction over our heads and there, hurtling along at fantastic speeds, turning and twisting off at the many signed junctions we could see cars, lorries, vans, in a non-stop ribbon of colour plus the squeal of tyres, and engines roaring. Mind you, we had to crane our necks and look up and up and up.

We moored underneath Spaghetti Junction and took some film and slides of these transport systems, so many years apart, and then we started up again on our peaceful 2 mph journey past gas works, steel works and finally came to rest against a nice grassy bank where ragwort grew. We were outside an engineering factory with a bus depot and garage opposite but, surprisingly, little noise came from either. It wasn't until 5.30 am the next morning that the bus garage let us know it was alive when most of the engines were started up and put through their paces before the buses were driven out. However, it was a convenient mooring, once we found a hole in a fence to crawl through; there we were, less than a mile from the Bull Ring and the main shopping centre.

We could have got even nearer Birmingham if we had continued along the Birmingham and Fazeley, as that went straight to Farmers Bridge and Gas Street Basin, both in the centre of the city, but we had decided to explore that route later.

Birmingham was another city I had never visited before. I had read some articles and seen pictures of it but had not been impressed. We were three days there most of which I spent walking up and down streets and through numerous subways. Birmingham people have been overcome by the motor car and theirs is a city planned for the machine age. The cars use the open roads while pedestrians walk underground for miles. You really can get lost in these subways, trying to find which road you want to come out at.

Nor did I enjoy shopping in Birmingham as everything seemed to be cheap tawdry rubbish. The Bull Ring is a depressing place. I've walked round it on a bustling Saturday and an eerie empty Sunday and a sleepy Monday morning ... and whatever the day the place looks mucky, cigarette packets, spearmint wrappers, lolly sticks, they pile up on the staircases, outside shops on the pavements ... ugghh.

There are two places that would entice me back for a short while; first, the city museum where I spent a fascinating three hours and could easily have stayed the whole three days. I noticed in the china section a porcelain exhibit of some early Spode cups decorated with roses. The painting was similar to the rose decorations which were a traditional part of early working boats. Indeed, china from the Spode factories was one of the earliest of cargoes regularly carried by canal. I wonder if there is any connection between the boats and the china? Could it have been a boatman who saw the roses on the china and thought they would look pretty on his boat?

The second place to which I'd return is the stall in the downstairs market that sold crabs and crabs only – in every size and form. Whole crabs, crab claws, crab paste. It was the first time I had ever seen a sea food specialist. Most of the sea food stalls sell winkles, shrimps, cockles, whelks and crabs but this stall didn't seem to lose by specialising. I had to take my turn among many eager jostling customers.

Birmingham, however, gave Owen a chance to meet up with some musical buddies. In fact, within ten minutes of our first exploration of the outdoor market a ringing shout, of 'Owen' carried across the stalls and the crowds of shoppers. We turned and there, grinning by the side of his handbag stall, was a clarinet player we knew. It took just five minutes to arrange for Owen to play that night in a local jazz club.

I wasn't sorry when it was time for us to leave Birmingham. A few yards from our mooring at Bordesley, I managed to jam *Bix* in a lock. It took Owen plus two workmen from the factory to get the boat free. A car wheel had been submerged in the lock and the water drawn by our boat had caused it to bob to the surface between the walls of the lock and the boat, firmly wedging boat and wall together.

That was the beginning of five miles of polluted canal. The amount of rubbish we travelled through was appalling. Settees, armchairs, mattresses, motor bikes, scooters, prams and a macabre sight of headless dolls, dolls' legs, arms and torsos, all bobbing up to the boat and swishing against the side.

Then there was the rubbish we didn't see which wrapped itself around the propeller. Owen spent hours with his arms immersed in the water cutting through bed springs, rope, plastic, and in one case a length of garden fence still complete with chestnut palings. At times like this I wish we had a visitor staying with us, one who tells us how lucky we are to have such a happy, carefree life.

As we sailed through the debris, beneath derelict factories and crumbling disused wharves, I began to wonder how long it would be before we left behind the desolation wrought by our progressive society. The first place in the waterways guide that looked like a village had the pretty name of Catherine de Barnes. According to the guide, that was the only pretty thing about the place. But we moored there overnight and found it soothing and pleasant after the miserable surroundings of the past day or so. At least it was clean and quiet and it has an excellent bakery I would recommend to anyone.

I looked forward to a few days of relaxing rural boating ahead. Birmingham was well and truly behind us.

16

It was a lovely morning as we continued down the Grand Union Canal towards Knowle Locks and the well maintained flight were a joy to work through. A helpful lock-keeper riding his small truck up and down the towpath was a welcome companion. Not that we were alone, for it was Saturday and swarms of visitors were watching the comings and goings of the boats using the locks. The surrounding countryside is much our kind of wallpaper, lush and green with perfect vistas of England at her best.

The hedges were hawthorn and full of blossom and my winemaking nose began to twitch. Back on the farm, I had had a regular routine for my winemaking. Starting with elder-flower, I went through the seasons as the fruits and flowers bloomed all over the farm. I made strawberry, raspberry, morello cherry, gooseberry, apple, plum, elderberry and finally blackberry.

It was one of the things I thought I'd have to give up when moving on to the boat, but I had brought along a couple of gallon jars just in case ... and now I was glad that I had them.

It seemed a waste to let that lovely hawthorn blossom fall to the ground and, although I had never before made wine from hawthorn, I decided to try. We picked and picked the small delicate heads and by coffee time they were in the first stages of their transformation in a plastic bucket alongside the food store.

We used the bikes that afternoon to visit Packwood House and gardens. It was a pleasant ride, about three miles, through fairly quiet country lanes. The smallish house was delightful with homely rooms, not grand lofty ones, the sort that a family would use each day to eat in or relax and look out over the garden with its splendid collection of yew trees laid out to represent the Sermon on the Mount. As you stroll beneath their tall and gracious boughs you follow a path that takes you up and up, until you reach the final, grand old yew – The Master.

The following day, we reached a formidable flight of locks whose name had gone before them. Almost all boaters we had met said, 'just wait until you have to do the Hatton Flight – 21 locks and a couple more after that before you get to Warwick!'

The locks here are the wide type so we usually waited a while to see if anyone else arrived. This helped to save water, of course, but today we hoped it would save some wear and tear on Owen's muscles.

It was obviously our lucky day for not only did a boat join us, but it was one belonging to a member of the Advisory Committee of the Inland Waterways Association, John Atkinson. He had his daughter and her friend as crew and they were very well trained indeed. If it hadn't been for the strong winds that accompanied us the whole way through, it would have been more fun than work. As it was, we had a much more enjoyable afternoon than we had anticipated.

John has a ship's bell on the top of his boat and a pair of binoculars around his neck. Once we were in the first lock, his crew ran ahead and prepared the next lock for us.

John watched through his binoculars and when the gates opened ahead, he rang the bell. His crew then went on to the next lock while we left one lock and chugged ahead to the ready and waiting next one, leaving Owen to close the gates behind us and see us through the next lock. And so it continued for the next three hours.

We had a welcome coffee break on board *Bix* afterwards and John was very impressed with our home, 'the ultimate' in boating, he called it.

That evening, we walked into Warwick and treated ourselves to a good meal at The Crown. Warwick itself we missed, because it was dark when we had finished dinner and the next morning we set off early to Royal Leamington Spa, three miles further along the canal. The approach to this once fasionable watering place is dreary indeed. A great deal of industry clings to the canal side, much of it made up of smallish firms who consider the canal a bottomless pit into which they can jettison their unwanted leftovers. However we spent a pleasant morning shopping in the town, happy to see many of the 18th century houses still standing.

Not far from Leamington Spa, we admired a pretty lock cottage at Welsh Road Lock, mooring a little further on, opposite a pub with the intriguing name of the Blue Lias. After dinner, that evening we walked to the pub for a drink and to satisfy our curiosity over the name. As we approached the pub we had another surprise, for there standing in the car park was an aeroplane.

Inside the welcoming bar, we learned that Blue Lias is the name of a stone quarried locally and secondly that the landlord is an ex-test-pilot, the Vampire plane being a somewhat costly souvenir of his past career.

Next morning we worked through the Stockton Locks a couple of hundred yards further up the canal accompanied by another narrow boat. By the time we had come to the end of these eight locks we were all on very friendly terms indeed and John and Lily invited us on board for coffee. They had a lovely boat. John was rebuilding the inside himself and although it was only partially completed it already had a comfortable, relaxing atmosphere, which came from the beautiful wood panelling in the dining area and galley.

We soon found out that John and Lily were the inhabitants of the pretty Welsh Road Lock cottage we had admired. They made us feel envious as they recounted their story. After retirement, they had spent three years searching for their dream cottage where they had both settled down to a quiet rural life, in contrast to teaching in Manchester. Lily appreciated her large garden and the canal views from her windows. John had plenty to do on the boat but, every now and again, they succumbed to the urge to travel for a few days when they just locked the cottage, untied the boat and set off.

In fact, that had happened this very morning. They didn't know how far they would be going, or whether they would be away from home for a day or a week. As they talked about the advantages and disadvantages of living by the canal, Owen and I sat and listened, hoping that one day we too would find a comparable cottage. Before saying goodbye, we promised 'to knock on the door whenever working through the lock,' and this we have done on a couple of occasions. Now that I have seen the inside of their home, I envy them even more.

We worked through Calcutt Locks together before separating at Napton Junction, they bound for Braunston while we headed back to Oxford and the River Thames.

Our trip along the Oxford canal was lively. We met many hirers of whom a surprisingly large number were Americans, some combining a boating holiday to Oxford, where they picked up a car to tour the Cotswolds.

One American couple we met were staying for two years. He was studying our social history and in reading about the canals they had both become fascinated by them and had booked a week's holiday.

We met them on their first day out and it was obvious that when it came to mooring they hadn't a clue. First of all, she jumped off without the rope, then he tried throwing the stern rope and it missed (it always does!). By now he had turned off his engine and was drifting about the canal. Eventually, with Owen giving instructions from the towpath, they safely tied up astern.

Later that evening, our neighbour came along to ask Owen to write down the instructions he had given. To our disgust, we learned that the boatyard from which they had hired the boat had given no instruction about handling the boat, or any details of the canals, locks or bridges. By the time we got to Banbury, we heard similar tales about this boatyard from other hirers, most American and Canadian. But once their teething troubles were over, they all seemed to enjoy their boating holidays. It doesn't reflect much credit on the boatyard, however.

At Cropredy, by now a home from home to us, we met *The Butt of Malmsey*, owned by a young Indian doctor who was taking out a colleague and his wife for their first boating trip. We met for dinner in a local inn and they all came back on *Bix* for coffee afterwards. Both doctors came from the hospital in East Grinstead noted for its work in plastic surgery ... what a relaxing change life on the boat must make after such arduous work.

'HP' as our young Indian doctor was called, advised us against the Thames but I told him that we knew it well and after years of exploring almost every part of it in hire boats, we were determined to take *Bix* on it. He stressed the differences I would find from the canals. The Thames was so crowded, he said. This we knew already; hadn't we been up and down it for almost 30 years? In fact, I had been born beside it at Greenwich and with my father and uncles all Thames bargebuilders, lightermen, and watermen, there wasn't much I didn't know about it. And the nearer we drew to Oxford and the river, the more excited I became ... A great believer in roots, I already felt the stirrings inside me as we approached mine.

17

We entered the Thames through Osney Lock, via a small backwater which runs under Oxford station. This route includes a railway bridge, two feet above the water. Thankfully, it is not used much by British Rail and remains open most of the time. When it is used, however, it takes four men to open and close it. No wonder it became notorious in the days of frequent rail services across it.

To navigate the River Thames, we needed another licence as *Bix* is licensed by the BWB only for the canals and waterways under their jurisdiction. Before we could obtain this licence, an official of the Thames Water Authority checked and inspected the boat to ensure that not only was it safe to take on the river, but that we also complied with sanitary and fire regulations. The inspection was carried out efficiently and in a friendly manner. A 14 day-licence cost us £12. Licences can be obtained for a day, a week, or any length of time up to 12 months.

After the canals it seemed a completely new world ... there were boats galore, everywhere you looked. River cruisers, ocean going craft, canoes, rowing boats, the powered craft moving at fantastic speeds. The speed limit on the Thames is double that of the canals, eight miles an hour but after the leisurely pace of our past few months, we seemed to be surrounded by power-crazy youngsters.

Despite its drawbacks, the Thames still has a magnetic charm for me. For the next two weeks, as we sailed past Abingdon, Clifton Hampden, Wallingford, Pangbourne, Cookham, Maidenhead and many other riverside towns and villages, I recalled holidays when our family were young.

Our conversation was continually interrupted as we came across favourite mooring places. 'Do you remember how well Marny steered the boat here when she was about ten?' and, 'look there's the place where we had a midnight swim,' and so on as we cruised down memory lane.

It was a good thing that we did have so much to reminisce over as no one seemed to want to talk to us. Boat-owners, with one exception, looked askance at our narrow boat. 'What the hell do you mean, bringing a canal boat on to the Thames?' one woman shouted at us. Nor did they realise that we could not moor or turn as easily or quickly as they could in their floating gin-palaces. Often, although it was obvious that we were going to tie up, one of them would nip along smartly and pinch the only available place for our length. No word of apology, not even a look in our direction. And then one day, two people on a boat spoke to us. Guess what; yes, they were on a narrow boat.

We were about to moor at Cookham when a 30 foot cruiser overtook us, turned on a sixpence under our nose and went into the spot we were aiming for. He found himself faced by the owner of narrow boat *Puffin* ahead, tied up there, who told him in no uncertain terms to find somewhere else.

The owners of *Puffin* shared our problems. They belonged to a boating club on the river some of whose members had not spoken to them since they had sold their small cruiser and bought the 40 foot narrow boat.

Cookham draws me like a magnet. Amongst its antique shops along the High Street pavement, is a real Aladdin's cave of treasures. Here, many years ago, on the first afternoon of a boating weekend I discovered a dark corner made even murkier by piles and piles of dusty books. By the time I'd read a bit of this one and decided I must buy that one, an unamused husband told me that it was now too damned dark to move the boat any further that day and I, guiltily, got up from amidst those dear friends piled higgledy, piggledy, dusted myself down and as a penance bought only one of the many 'must-haves', a beautiful red suede-covered copy of Tennyson for 2s. 6d.

Now, all those years later, I ran past the Stanley Spencer Gallery to see if my book hidey-hole was still there, and bless you Cookham ... it was. So I foraged ... but once again bought only one book for now the problem is space and I've already added to the strict ration of books I was allowed to bring aboard *Bix*. But I just had to add the William Harrison Ainsworth to my collection, not a popular Victorian author, I know, but I prefer him to Dickens and now have more of his books than any other author with me on board.

As much as we would have liked to stay and take a more leisurely view of the Thames, our licence expired after two weeks. As we progressed down river through the more built-up areas of Chertsey, I began to feel that perhaps the canals did have a something extra to offer. They are certainly more relaxing, even if you do have to work yourselves through the locks.

But it was the Thames locks that made us feel welcome. Without exception the lock-keepers showed interest in *Bix*. If we didn't speak to boaters, we certainly did to lock-keepers.

A different technique is needed when using the larger Thames locks. The lock-keepers tell you when to enter and where to go, the boat held by her ropes to prevent banging other craft, engine turned off, all new to us canal users. Owen did most of the steering on the Thames while I obeyed the lock-keepers' commands.

One lock-keeper called. 'I say, she's a beauty. We haven't seen her before,' meaning *Bix*, not me I hasten to add. Once we were inside the lock, he chatted away about the canals. An ex-working boatman himself who had carried coal along the canals, he obviously missed them still. Another keeper recognised the style of the boat-builder who had constructed *Bix* and so it went on down river. One assistant keeper even called out, 'yours is the best narrow boat we've ever seen. Come again.'

While we had these friendly chats with the lock-keepers, most of the other craft owners showed only impatience, one even told the keeper to 'hurry up a bit, I'm in a rush.' It had little effect on our man who, in fact, was waiting for another boat to reach the lock. 'For some people there seems to be no tomorrow,' he said.

The glorious summer weather continued throughout the trip and we more than made up for lost bathing time. Owen and I both love swimming and, of course, the river scores here over the canals. We swam before breakfast and lunch most days and at Clifton Hampden I think most of the villagers were in the water that afternoon.

That famous inn, The Barley Mow, at Clifton Hampden is still unchanged, one of the rare 'cruck-buildings,' a method of construction dating back nearly 2,000 years. It consisted of bending over pairs of trees to form arches, setting a ridge pole on top and filling in the framework. In early times they didn't bother with the filling in. But the Barley Mow has walls, thick ones to exclude river mists and to keep you cool on hot days. It is one of the places mentioned by Jerome K Jerome in *Three men in a boat.* When we visited the pub in the sixties, I was disappointed to find that the landlord did not speak with a strong Oxfordshire accent, but was in fact Welsh. However, he was a warm and hospitable landlord.

On this visit in 1975, I had an even greater surprise. The familiar rooms with their cosy cushions and low beams to catch strangers had not altered, the food as good as ever, the landlord's greeting was still warm but this time it came from a Greek!

A few days later we moored outside a somewhat older and even more famous historic building – Hampton Court Palace. We arrived on a sunny Sunday afternoon to a bustling throng of sightseers promenading through the palace grounds and towpath. Our long narrow steel boat caused a stir of excitement as we nosed slowly along looking for a mooring.

Sitting in our lounge later that evening, we were amused to overhear comments about us. 'Oh yes, she's French. See, it's got its telephone number, just beneath the name. That's a Paris code.' This conveyer of misinformation was describing our licence transfer for the Thames! Our Paris telephone numbers read 0-12-75 which translated 0 for Osney, the 12th licence issued in 1975!

Another know-all's voice came down to us authoritatively. 'This is a 12 berth, I know it well. It's hired out regularly, about £100 per week.' Owen wanted to go on deck and bet him a fiver he could not find the other eight berths, but I drew more amusement from sitting quietly in the cabin and listening.

The next day saw the start of Wimbledon so, of course, we had the first rain for almost a month. We continued down river towards Teddington, our last lock, in really heavy squalls. Here we had to check the times of the tides, for after Teddington the Thames is tidal. We had two locks to navigate on the River Brent at Brentford, where we were leaving the Thames, which operate for only a couple of hours either side of high water. From the River Brent, we met up with the Grand Union Canal once again.

As there are virtually no mooring facilities on this part of the Thames it is essential you time this bit of navigation correctly. However we safely found the entrance to the River Brent which, with the locks, is not well defined or easy to navigate when approaching from up river.

So it was with relief I greeted the Brentford lock-keeper. Once again we were back on familiar canal territory. Past Brentford station we moored in a surprisingly tranquil spot, no more than a mile from busy Brentford High Street, and on the edge of Osterley Park.

Before we had finished tying up, we heard three little boys of about eight or nine years of age comment on our boat. Their apparent leader, his grubby face smiling a welcome said, 'coo, what a smashing boat. We're the Watermill Gang, I'm Hercules.' And pointing to his two equally grubby companions he went on, 'he's Crackers and that's the Professor.'

We duly introduced ourselves and over glasses of lemon squash and biscuits, I was let into the secrets of the gang's fishing expeditions, camping sites, their favourite dens, and many others I'm not allowed to share with you.

I felt really happy and relaxed. I knew I was back on the canals without any map to tell me.

18

The canal atmosphere soon encompassed us, welcoming us like alumni returning to the fold.

We were on familiar ground but in unfamiliar waters. As London landlubbers we knew well the places we were passing: but Brentford offers a different face to the canal from that which it shows to the High Street, despite the enormous warehouse that straddles the canal here.

We soon reached Hanwell Locks with their historic variety of bridges for the eye to linger on, a lovely old iron bridge dating back to 1820 or maybe a warm red brick bridge to help countrify the canal.

We moored outside Southall to shop. The sun blazed from a cloudless sky on a mass of gorgeous Indian women in bright saris, for all the world as if we were in Bombay. Most shops sold Indian food and the post office and bank had Indian clerks to deal with their own countrymen.

Eager to try new food, I bought an Indian sweetmeat made of almond paste, mixed with nuts, angelica and cherries. It was delicious and that evening I wished that I had had the nerve to buy and wear a sari as I ate my supper. I had been sorely tempted by the price: a lovely one in ice-blue costing less then £3. It would have kept me cooler than the disreputable old shorts and sun top I have worn for so long.

During the day we travelled through busy industrial areas, but at night the moorings were surprisingly peaceful. I became so used to waving back to people in factories, gasworks, and offices that it came as a surprise to turn off along the Paddington arm and discover dozens of anglers at Alperton, near Horsdenden Hill, a rural oasis in this factory-orientated part of London.

Next day we cruised over the top of the North Circular Road at Park Royal. Shortly after crossing this aqueduct we skirted the back of Wormwood Scrubs, an expanse of wilderness separating us.

We moored for lunch outside Kensal Green cemetery and could see the tops of ornate tombstones peeping over the long, brick wall. Again, the canal is so peaceful that office workers from nearby Harrow Road are attracted to eat by the canal side. After our meal we had unexpectedly to rescue a pigeon from drowning. The poor bird had been trying to drink from the canal but the towpath was rather too high and in he had toppled. Once out on the bank, he shook his wings and tamely drank from the dish of water I proffered.

We continued our journey high above the roofs of Kensal Town. From the boat we could look over the top of London and pick out well known spots including the Post Office Tower. That night we enjoyed an attractive mooring, the glittering lights on the ground competing with the Milky Way above.

Eventually we reached Little Venice, that part of the canal system everyone has heard about, and the one on which the BWB lavishes money. It is, of course, a well-known spot for the tourist trade and during the holiday season the BWB have a regular water-bus service which runs from Little Venice, where you board at the junction of the Paddington arm with the Regents Canal, through London Zoo, passing the Bird Aviary designed by Lord Snowdon, with pens of water buck opposite, and so to Camden Lock.

The boatmen in charge make it abundantly clear that theirs are the most important craft on the canal. In fact, it should be theirs exclusively judging by their behaviour. People like us are considered a nuisance so they speed by creating an enormous wash to rock the boat fiercely, all accompanied by shouts and insults.

Several houseboats are moored at Little Venice and although we stayed in and around this area for about a month, moving continuously between Camden Lock, Bethnal Green, and Little Venice, not once did we speak to the owners. Some had cultivated gardens by the side of the canal where people occasionally sat in deck chairs. We waved and greeted them but they felt it beneath them to acknowledge the presence of a boat that actually moved.

On arrival at Little Venice we contacted the BWB superintendent, Mr Andrews who allowed us to stay four days near Delamere Terrace, a handy mooring for shops and launderette in the nearby Harrow Road. We were less lucky with our Calor gas supply, however as the nearest place was outside Islington. They could not deliver so we had to await our son's visit by car to restock our gas supplies.

For three weeks we had a constant flow of visitors to *Bix*. Son-in-law popped in for lunch from his nearby office; an old friend found that we had moored near to his dentist so arrived for coffee after a brief check-up; and our son came to lunch and stayed two days.

We moved down past Cumberland Basin and through Camden Lock where a surprise awaited us: lock-keepers to work us through. In fact, we found that on the Regents Canal we were not allowed to work the locks which were padlocked after the lock-keeper had finished work for the day.

One visit that really pleased me was my mother's. At 83 years of age, she saw our new home for the first time. We had asked her to stay with us but she had always refused. 'I can't sleep on water,' she claimed. But now that we were within easy car distance from her flat she came to tea aboard and sailed through Maida Vale tunnel with us, enjoying every minute.

We were surprised to find so few boats using the Regents Canal. There are no boatyards hiring out as far as we could find and in six weeks we saw only one hire and two private boats. One of the latter named *Jonazark* moored behind us near Camden Lock. Boat names had become an in-joke with us by now and we often groaned aloud at some dreadful puns used like *Cantelpit*. Our neighbour's name was Jones, we found, hence the boat's name. They too lived aboard and cruised like us, except they disembarked at the end of the summer. They lived near Derby and each April they closed their house and took to the boat, planning no particular route and finding great joy and pleasure wherever they travelled. In the autumn they started back for home in time to join evening classes for the winter. A lovely way to spend a retirement.

The BWB and local councils have developed the towpath from Little Venice to Islington tunnel. The wide path has plenty of seats to encourage walkers and visitors, an excellent scheme. But, and it's a big but, each night the gates leading to the canal are locked so the occupants, moored on this stretch, cannot reach town for a meal, or anywhere else for that matter.

There is nothing on the towpath to inform the boat of this. Such notices are on the gates used by pedestrians! Which we discovered the hard way. After dinner on board, we decided to take a walk through Regents Park but like the animals in the zoo, a few yards from the boat, we were trapped!

The BWB explained that the gates had to be locked because of vandalism. It seemed strange to us after wandering around so many canals, winter and summer, to find it was only in this exclusive London area that they had to lock away the canal each night.

It seemed even stranger when two nights later, we tied up at Islington; an excellent mooring this, five minutes from the Angel tube station and up to 14 days' free mooring allowed. People strolled along the towpath and I soon got chatting to the regulars, including Harry, a council workman who sat in his little office by the side of the canal. Apart from unlocking the gate in the morning and locking it at night, he had only to watch for vandals.

Sad to say, his vigilant eye was unavailable one sunny Friday evening. We had been talking to a young couple, pushing their baby in a pram along the towpath. He was in the Army and stationed in barracks not far from the canal, near City Road. As we talked about our floating home and canals generally, it appeared that he too was an enthusiast and, in fact, when his service career was finished, he intended applying to the BWB for a job. We could have continued all night, but Harry arrived jingling his keys so we said goodnight. Owen and I sat at the front of our boat, surveying the now empty landscape and feeling like lepers as the public disappeared and the huge wooden gates closed. Then came the sound of a padlock, locking us in for the night.

As I was clearing away the coffee cups Owen put a finger to his lips. Over a gate appeared first one head, then another, followed by the rest of their bodies, until some five or six youths were running along the towpath towards the bridge.

Next we saw that they had crossed the canal and were climbing the fence of a factory in whose yard stood piles of paving stones and slabs of marble-like material. Owen called to ask them what they were doing. As they had no idea that someone was living on a boat, so close to them, the shock was tremendous. But not for long. Realising that we were on one side and they the other, the first thing they did was to throw stones at us, finally breaking one of the bedroom windows.

79

We tried to find a way across but couldn't discover their route, nor could we take the boat over as that would make it too vulnerable and of course, we couldn't get out to the road to seek help.

They knew this too and laughed as they piled marble and concrete into the canal. We stood helpless and watched hundreds of pounds' worth of material being tipped into the water.

'If only the gates were not locked,' I thought, 'we would still be talking to our young couple. There would be people around and the vandalism couldn't have occurred.' The locks keep out the good; the bad will get in if they wish, gates or no gates.

I was so incensed by this and the thought that our boat had received its first damage in this so-called protected canal area, that I wrote to the local paper and also carried on correspondence with the BWB in the *Times* diary. But I was checkmated. The BWB would only reiterate that the locks and police supervision were there to stop vandalism. On the day that the *Times* printed the BWB reply to my comment, one of the police who patrolled on a scooter stopped alongside *Bix* and said, 'good thing you weren't moored at Little Venice last night. Someone came along and cut all the ropes.' So what is the answer? All I can say is that no gates are locked in Birmingham, Coventry, Leicester, or Leamington Spa and I believe statistics show that the latter has one of the highest crime rates in the country!

But, of course, life wasn't all grin and bear it on the Regents Canal. We met some very interesting people and had two more of those 'coincidences.'

Whilst moored near Camden Lock, our son Jan spent some time with us. As we sat outside for lunch one day we could hear in the distance the day-trip boat *Jenny Wren* approaching. This boat passed four times a day and by now I knew not only the steerers and guides, but their commentary as well. As they passed, to Jan's amusement, I mouthed the words coming from the boat, 'sloping steps you see by the side of the canal were to aid horses back on to the towpath after they had fallen in ...' I explained to Jan how often I'd heard those words, when a loud American voice yelled out, 'There's *Bix*, my god, it's *Bix*.' I turned to find all the passengers of *Jenny Wren* staring at us while, halfway down the boat, two figures leaned perilously over the side. It was Len and Paula, the two Americans we had shown how to tie up when they were in trouble on the Oxford Canal.

We had a joyous reunion when their trip came to an end and they came on board for a cup of tea. They were still so enthusiastic about their canal holiday that they had brought a visiting brother and sister-in-law on this day trip to give them an idea of what it was like, but Len had to agree that the Regents Canal is rather gimmicky and compares unfavourably with the rest of the system.

Another day, I was busy inside the boat when I heard a bell ringing. We were moored by the side of Delamere Terrace and I thought it was probably a bicycle bell, but as it continued louder and louder I realised that I'd heard that sound before. I went on deck and there coming serenely towards us was John Atkinson on *Mary Jane*, his ship's bell ringing and swinging on the top of his boat as it had when we'd joined him working through the Hatton Flight.

It was sheer chance that had brought him to Little Venice. He was on his way to Uxbridge to drop off two friends who were flying from Heathrow, a bus ride away. We had time for a cool glass of lager whilst he re-told his friends about meeting us. Before they left, he asked permission to show them over our boat. 'It's still the ultimate,' he said.

With the weather still gloriously hot, I took to doing my daily chores on deck. One afternoon, as I sat shucking peas, a woman whom I'd seen before on several occasions, passed by. She was very attractive and usually wore long flowing skirts and often, as today, she was knitting as she walked.

Today, she stopped to talk. Eventually she came on board and expressed surprise on being taken over our luxurious home. She thought *Bix* would interest her husband and when she said that they lived about 100 yards down the towpath, I invited them over for drinks that evening. And that's how we met the well-known writer, Mervyn Jones, and his wife Jeanne. We soon found that Jeanne and I had been involved with the Greenwich theatre. Jeanne was the wardrobe mistress in its early years and I had belonged to the Society of Friends and helped with publicity. Strangely, we had never met.

Jeanne suggested that we might like to move the boat nearer to their back entrance, but I decided to stay put as it was only for one more day and, in any case, I had a splendid view from my bedroom of a lovely garden perched high up on the embankment. It contained masses of wrought iron work and statues, a lovely picture to which to awake.

Jeanne agreed that it was an interesting garden. 'But,' she added 'I don't know if Clive Jenkins likes your mooring at the bottom of his garden.' Well Mr Jenkins, we didn't tie up to your trees and we're sorry if we caused any inconvenience.

One of our breakfasts on the Regents Canal was the highlight of our stay. I had been sending bits and pieces to the Today programme for years, since the days when Jack de Manio introduced the programme. During our travels on *Bix*, I continued to send these to John Timpson who had used one or two.

I told John we were coming to London and how about sampling a breakfast on *Bix* as a change from the BBC canteen. The reply was not only prompt, but alarming. My letter had gone around the whole team and they all accepted! I was to telephone when we arrived and arrange a day for the visit with one of John's colleagues, Trevor Taylor. This was a pleasant piece of news as I had known Trevor when we both worked on BBC Medway.

The day duly arrived and although I had warned Trevor about our limited space, I wondered how many to cater for. Thank goodness, it was a warm bright morning and we could breakfast outside in the front well of the boat. I made a batch of wholewheat rolls, a large bowl of yoghurt, boiled eggs, and a dish of muesli, plus jugs of freshly ground coffee.

John, Trevor and a couple of other colleagues arrived shortly after the programme went off air and in no time at all we were eating, drinking and chatting away like old friends. John had a boat and Trevor worked on a boating magazine programme on BBC Medway, so we had a mutual interest. I'm sorry to say that we talked so much that we almost let the night editor fall overboard. He had been sitting on the edge of the boat, holding a cup of coffee after working all night, so was more inclined to sleep than chat. The warm sun, hot coffee and gentle movement as we rocked in the water caused by the operation of Camden Lock caused him to close his eyes and nod off. It was John who noticed his night editor leaning further and further over. It was obviously time to finish breakfast: I didn't want to be responsible for the loss of a BBC producer.

This was our last day on the Regents Canal and as we said goodbye to John and his friends, we heard a shout and Jeanne came out of her gate running down the towpath. 'Glad I caught you,' she said, and handed me a pot of rosemary. A lovely present – rosemary for remembrance. We will certainly remember Jeanne, Mervyn and the lock-keeper living in Islington who taught the starling to speak, plus all the many other friends of the Regents Canal. We will be back.

19

By now it was August, in the middle of a heatwave. If Owen and I had enjoyed our travels so far, we were, during the following week, to find a lot more happiness and fun for we had our two eldest grandchildren holidaying with us.

It may sound strange to say that we had, and did, everything that one should have and do on a holiday considering that for most of the time we were only ten miles from the centre of London. We boated, swam, fished, walked, picnicked, watched cricket and, to Dylan's delight, spent half a day at London airport watching the planes come and go.

Erica proved to be an apt pupil at steering *Bix* and for most of the time she was to be found alongside Owen at the back of the boat. Dylan preferred to be in front with me where we could bird-watch. On one glorious afternoon at Widewater lock, Harefield, we had a competition to see who could spot the most dragonflies. They were prolific along this stretch, large orange ones as well as the more common blue, and an even larger species that was chocolate brown.

At Uxbridge we moored and took a bus to London airport where we baked in the midday sun on the roof and watched the antics of the plane spotters who appear to have formed themselves into a mysterious club. They sit in corners or lie on the ground with transistor radios pressed tightly to their ears, the long aerials waving wildly above them. Both Erica and Dylan were fascinated by the crowds, the noise and the excitement whenever a plane in the livery of a rare air line was cleared for landing. But we began to wilt in the heat and gratefully returned to the calmer and cooler atmosphere of the canal in the afternoon.

Once past the Slough Arm, the canal is rural, even Rickmansworth, which seems to be surrounded by water. The rivers Colne, Chess and Gade flow through or near its boundaries. Then there is the canal itself, plus the Rickmansworth aquadrome ... two lakes where all kinds of water sports are available.

The River Gade becomes canalised for a stretch at Rickmansworth and once again most of the local youngsters made use of the flowing part of the canal for swimming. We moored for the night at the junction of the river and canal and swam before breakfast next morning.

I suggested to Erica and Dylan that if they kept a log-book, like all good sailors, they would have something to show their parents. So every morning, after breakfast, they sat down to write up the previous day's adventures.

I had stapled together some sheets of paper and each day they wrote on the top half and drew a picture along the bottom. After this, both had to practice the piano (strict instructions from their mother to me) thereafter the day was free for whatever they fancied.

Erica, Dylan and I had a secret to keep during their week's stay. It was Owen's birthday on Saturday and the three of us decided to surprise him with a party. We would not give him our presents or cards until the evening meal, which, of course, would be a special one.

How Dylan got through that day I don't know. If he hadn't been able to run to me to go over and over again just what we were going to do, I think he would have burst.

At last, the moment arrived. Erica beamed and Dylan squealed with delight as Owen was made to sit down and do nothing while he was served with drinks and nuts. Then, poor man, with handfuls of these, his presents were thrust upon him. 'Open them now to see if you like them,' they cried. And he did. A toothbrush was definitely what he wanted and he loved the bar of crystalised apricot, his very favourite fruit.

In fact, he was so pleased with his party that he promised to take us out for a slap-up meal the next night, which was to be the children's last with us.

We spent the day leisurely chugging through Abbots Langley, and then Kings Langley, passing the Ovaltine factory beyond which we could see their model farm, looking just like a toy model. There were many anglers along the banks and when Dylan excitedly pointed out the fish swimming by the side of the boat, I could well understand the reason why there were so many busily fishing.

Never before have I seen such huge fish, except on a fishmonger's slab. Hearing the yells from our boat one angler grinned across at us knowing full well what was causing the excitement. I wonder if the fish feed on waste from the Ovaltine factory? There must be something in this piece of water to cause them so to thrive.

Hemel Hempstead was the sad and final stop for the children. We moored by the side of the local cricket club ground where a game was in progress. After a quick lunch Owen and Dylan watched the rest of the game while Erica and I went into town to seek out a restaurant for our evening meal.

Our night out was great fun. We had found a Chinese restaurant where Dylan enjoyed the handful of prawn crackers that came with our aperitifs and decided he would like a bowl of them for his meal, with a large Pepsi. Erica showed her two years' superiority and asked for advice on the dishes that took her fancy, before giving her order. It was a lovely evening and a perfect ending to a happy week. We had had to change our whole pattern of boating life for the children and we'd loved every minute of it.

20

Each day brought something new into our lives, sometimes a place came along which we could not miss. That's how I felt about the Aylesbury Arm which leads off the Grand Union at Marsworth.

Our journey through Berkhamsted had been pleasant. It was here that I spent more than an hour one morning watching mother moorhen getting into quite a fluster as she tried to prepare her nest for another brood, plagued as she was by the youngsters of the previous one.

It paralleled so many human situations. The youngsters wanted to play while she had work to do. She constantly swam into the reeds for fresh supplies for the nest, followed by her four well-grown chicks who always found something better than the reeds to play with. One even brought her the glittering ring from a beer can. She squawked indignantly and administered several blows from her gaudy red and yellow beak. These they tried to avoid by popping beneath the surface only to re-appear with bedraggled weeds dripping from their still grey beaks.

At Marsworth, we moored near the reservoirs desperately reduced by the hot summer, as was the canal level. We had experienced trouble several times in mooring and now had to use the gangplank on most days.

Owen was booked for a week's summer school of music and I planned to look after six-month-old Benjamin while his parents, Marny and Keith, took a short holiday. They arrived at Marsworth on Sunday and stayed a day before going on to Wales. I suggested a trip in the boat along the Aylesbury Arm before they left which pleased them.

I had already walked the stretch and found it both beautiful and tranquil: perfect country scenery, miles and miles of fields, trees, dotted by a farm here and there, where I actually heard and saw a nightingale one afternoon. Most of the surrounding land belongs to the Rothschild estate and it looks today very much the same as it did when the navvies first dug the canal. In several places, I could forget I lived in the 20th century ... no pylons, no major roads, no traffic. The canal-side plants were thick and lush, reaching to heights not normally seen in England – more like a tropical forest growth: rose-bay willow herb for instance stood more than seven feet high.

This was an ideal cruise for Marny and Keith with 16 locks to navigate.

Keith will not mind if I say that he is not the kind of crew I would choose if others were available as he has little or no experience of boating. Marny, on the other hand, has always had a practical mind and since she learned to drive our small farm tractor when she was about eight years old, she has always been happy tinkering with mechanical equipment. But Marny was now a mother and busy inside the boat with Benjamin and so it was that with me at the tiller and Keith crewing we left Marsworth early next morning.

I had no worries for I'd been handling *Bix* now for 10 months and knew that the Aylesbury Arm held no problems. The first two locks are staircase locks. That is, one leads directly into the other. I shouted out instructions to Keith as I manoeuvred our 6 feet 10 inches into the narrow seven foot lock and away we went. We entered the second lock Keith opened the paddles, down went the boat, he opened the bottom gates and off I started.

I'd got about four feet of *Bix* out of the lock when the boat inexplicably stopped, something that had not happened before. I reversed the engine and then tried to leave the lock again. This time we got a bit further, but to my horror the front of the boat seemed to be rising up and over the sill of the lock before coming to a halt.

Keith had no idea that something was wrong. How could he, it was the first time he'd seen a boat leaving a lock ... then I realised the problem. No water! I yelled to Keith, nine feet above me, to go back and open the paddles behind the boat which would allow the water to flow from the top lock into my lock. *Bix* then sailed out smoothly under a narrow bridge and on to locks three and four which are adjacent. Number three lock was OK but I ran out of water in the pound between it and number four. Poor Keith was now running back to lock number two opening up paddles, then going ahead to open up number four. Then once I was in, back to close number two before helping me through number four.

On leaving lock number four, we ran out of water again and I realised that we were embarked on a long, hazardous and tiring journey. I wondered if I could reverse the boat through all four locks back on to the main canal again and while considering this, I noticed a young man on a scooter stop and speak to Keith before continuing his journey towards the junction.

Keith went back to open the paddles of number three and as *Bix* gratefully floated again on water instead of mud, our scooter friend reappeared. He stopped and told me that he was the lock-keeper for the arm, that he had opened the top paddles of the first four locks and he would see that they so remained until we reached Aylesbury. He told Keith to keep all the future top paddles open which confused my apprentice crew, as I had instructed him always to close the paddles. How quickly the canal grapevine had got the message to the lock-keeper that some idiot woman was bringing a 65 foot boat down the arm.

We made progress, but oh so slowly and laboriously. *Bix* grounded every 200 yards or so and on one occasion she leaned over so much that I visualised my telling Owen he no longer had a home.

After a ten-minute lunch break, we continued with Keith walking, running, looking anxiously at *Bix*, operating locks, doing everything but enjoy tranquil boating, poor chap. It was nearly 7.30 pm when we reached the deeper waters of the Aylesbury basin. Although we had had only a snack lunch, we were too worn out to want much of an evening meal and were in bed by 9 pm exhausted. Thankfully, Benjamin proved a model baby and slept throughout the night.

Next morning things looked better. After all we had made it and a little excitement added spice to a boating trip. Marny and Keith left and I had a splendid week getting to know my newest grandchild. I remembered to write to Owen to let him know that *Bix* was now in Aylesbury. I wrote, 'your turn to steer back to Grand Union. I don't want you to miss any of the adventure.' That gave him something to think about.

During the week, I came to know the lock-keeper well as he lived aboard a boat moored near the basin. He explained that the canal had been re-opened only recently after being derelict for years and it really needed much more dredging but, like so much of the waterways system, it was a question of finance. Again, I wondered why so many people are eager to re-open more of our disused canals when we already have 2,000 miles which the BWB find impossible to supervise and maintain to a reasonable standard.

I realise, of course, what an exciting achievement it must be to see a stretch of canal come alive again, but what happens after a year of so when the weeds have overgrown, dredging is not possible for at least another two years, and the locals have rediscovered what is to them a bottomless pit for their rubbish.

But to return to Aylesbury, a delightful town. Every day I pushed Benjamin's pram around the shops or the park; so cleverly have the developers planned their new shopping precinct that it wasn't until my last day that I found out that they had one!

It was with regret that I handed Benjamin back to Marny. I had enjoyed looking after him and although on the second day I had lost his mum's carefully worked-out timetable and diet sheet, I found that my old skills weren't entirely lost, only kept in the background.

Owen duly arrived at Aylesbury and I recounted my adventures. He listened, amused I think at my daring to take the boat on my own, well at least without him, but I don't think he really believed it was as bad as I made out.

He changed his mind within half an hour of leaving the basin. Not only did we have a water shortage, but we got something caught round the propeller as we were entering a lock. With the aid of my sharp carving knife, Owen started to hack through some black rubber material which had wrapped itself round and round our propeller. He brought handfuls of it up and eventually, to the surprise of the Sunday afternoon strollers, who were watching us, he retrieved the bottom half of a diver's suit. Who on earth would use that in these waters? When there is water in this section, it can only be three feet at the deepest. Just another problem that goes with opening up derelict canals, I suppose.

We thankfully re-entered the main line of the Grand Union and as it was nearly 7 p.m., we decided to stay moored near the junction. The following morning, we were picking up our mail from Marsworth post office, a few hundred yards along the towpath. As for tonight, well the White Lion was all of 20 yards from our home and they advertised Evening Dinners ... so we sampled one and very good it was too. I thought we deserved it after the trials and tribulations of the Aylesbury Arm behind us. Tomorrow we could look forward to easier waters; well, that's what I thought.

21

It was a warm sunny morning when Owen went off along the towpath to collect our mail. Marsworth's is one of the rare post offices situated by the side of the canal, an attrative cottage and garden with a general store attached.

It was still warm and sunny when Owen returned so we sat in the front well of the boat to catch up with our news. Owen passed a letter over to me and within seconds I was shivering – with fear.

The letter was from the small company in which we had once had shares. They had been sold but we had loaned them £3,000 which was being paid back at £100 per month. We charged no interest on the loan for sentimental reasons as this was a company we had started ourselves in a very small way some 30 years earlier. The new owners now wrote to inform us that due to increased overheads, inflation, and a drop in sales they were going into liquidation. They would not be able to repay any more of the loan.

It was as if a bubble which had encapsulated us had burst and we felt again the cold air of the outside world. We relied upon this money as our sole income and had tailored our life to this £25 per week on which we had managed very well. After buying *Bix* we had invested the balance of the farm sale in such a way that we could not touch it for two years which yielded a high interest. This in turn was invested by our bank as a hedge against inflation.

Suddenly, on a bright summer's day, we were living on a luxurious floating home, with not a penny's income on which to live. My mind flashed back to our previous secure, comfortable farm with food, friends, family, warmth and a good income. In 1973, Owen and I brought in about £70 per week. Farm overheads had swallowed a large proportion but we were quite comfortable and I never looked to see if I had any money left in my purse by Thursday.

What were we going to do now? We could write to our accountant and to the company directors for more details, but that didn't help our immediate financial situation. Our bank balance showed about £30 in hand. Certainly we would have to continue to live on *Bix* as we had no other home and it was not only cheaper to live on a boat, but we just couldn't give up *Bix*, not yet anyway. Obviously our dream of a two-year sabattical was over: we decided to get jobs.

That night we assessed our abilities. I could type, write articles, lecture, cook, look after children, do any housework. Owen was a musician, lecturer, writer, farmer and had management experience. Between us, we had quite a bit to offer; if not top bracket at least there was variety.

We wrote letters to every college of further education, summer school, adult education centre. In fact, we wrote more than 100 letters offering our services as lecturers and teachers in jazz. If anything came of these, it would not be until next year, as we knew from the half a dozen we were tied up with that all courses were arranged a year in advance.

Immediate work had to be obtained and in any form. We decided to move the boat eight miles down to Leighton Buzzard, the nearest town of any size.

As the canal meandered past Slapton, we crossed and recrossed the borders of Bedfordshire and Buckinghamshire before reaching Linslade, using waterways maps as well as ordnance survey maps to give us some idea how near we were to roads and bus routes. At Linslade we realised that we were now passing close to the scene of the great train robbery. If this story had been fiction, we would have found the sacks of money caught up in our propeller, been rewarded and our troubles would have been over.

But the truth is that we tied up near the bridge which is at the end of Leighton Buzzard high street. Here was a small community of boats, some with people living on board: it was nice to have neighbours once more. We tied up behind two coal boats and were surprised to see how many people came at weekends to buy coal direct from the barges.

A water point and sanitary station near to our mooring suggested that if we stayed a couple of weeks or so with temporary jobs, this would be an ideal spot.

After 'inflation' the next word on every news bulletin was 'unemployment', but, undeterred, we systematically went through Leighton Buzzard looking for work. Owen's first visit to the Department of Employment was a bit off-putting. When asked his address he replied, 'I live on a boat.' 'Oh, you're a vagrant,' came the clerk's reply!

However, we scanned the local newspaper, advertisements in shop windows, and I registered with a temp agency. I had to take a typing test and to my surprise they praised me which made me wonder about the standards of their other clients.

It took me five days to find a job: part-time kitchen help at the local conservative club for 50p an hour, but only 10 minutes walk from the boat. I felt nervous applying for the job; was I too old, would they want a water-gipsy working for them? My employers turned out to be a young couple. He was the steward attending to the bar and the dining room while his wife did the catering. I helped out in the kitchen as general dogsbody for four days a week at lunch times.

Owen and I knew that our boat licence did not allow us to stay as residents anywhere on the canal and we would have to move the boat every few days or so. We thought that if both could get jobs for six to eight weeks at a time, we could save enough to cover our move to another town. I suggested we tried to live off £15 per week and save the rest.

Owen cycled around the local farms asking for work and on the eighth day found full-time employment on a chicken farm in Slapton.

We felt proud when at the end of the second week, we brought home about £35 between us. Income tax was stopped on an emergency code, of course, and we looked forward to the time when we would receive our rebate on this.

Life took on a completely new tempo. Could it be that our lazy leisurely travels of the past months had slowed us down? I don't think so, but we both knew that we would never again recapture those sometimes magical months, months when we had grown closer together and had somehow felt reborn to a world awaiting discovery.

At the weekends, we moved the boat back to Slapton, or on towards Soulbury or Fenny Stratford. I grew to love the peace of the canal around Slapton, with a backdrop of the Dunstable downs and its white lion cut out in the chalk advertising Whipsnade zoo. When the weather conditions were right, there would be the occasional surprise appearance of a hot air balloon floating over the top of the hills. Gliders too performed quiet acrobatics above our heads.

We stayed eight weeks at our jobs ... moving up and down the canal a couple of miles one way, then a couple of miles the other. If it was too far for us to walk to work we cycled.

I got to know many of the shopkeepers in Linslade and found out that Little Italy would be a more appropriate name for the town as a genuine Italian community has sprung up here. Often you meet Italian grandma with her grandchildren shopping and it's a little one asking the prices because Grandma doesn't speak English. So we tried different pastas, wines and cheeses and I was always given a piece of cheese or ham to taste before buying.

By the time we were ready to leave, we knew that life was going to be quite an adventure for us during the next 18 months or so as we struggled to exist on £15 a week.

We had no hesitation about trying to make a living wherever we stopped, now we had cleared the first hurdle. And while we moved about, I could get down to serious freelance writing, something I did not relish, as I think it's one of the most soul-destroying professions. But needs must when the devil drives, so with £1 of my newly-earned wages, I bought a copy of my 'bible', *The Writers and Artists Yearbook* and settled down to work.

Owen, who had always been a self employed person, was unable to claim unemployment benefit and, because of our investments, we could not claim supplementary benefits, but so far in our lives, we have never depended on anyone but ourselves for a roof, food and clothes and we hope to continue in the same way.

I took a last walk along the River Ouzel which runs parallel to the canal at Leighton Buzzard. As if they were putting on a special show for me, that afternoon a pack of goldfinches charmed me with their dance and song as they pecked at the thistle seed heads; dabchicks dived and bobbed up again along by my side and when I sat down to say a quiet thanks to Someone Somewhere for showing us we could still survive, a stoat suddenly appeared, strolling leisurely on the opposite bank. Just as leisurely, it seemed, a water vole was patrolling his own particular trade route, which unfortunately took him right in front of the stoat. With one quick nip the stoat had the vole firmly held by the back of the neck. He then carried on, just as leisurely, presumably to have his tea ... and as I returned for mine, I cursed myself for not having the camera with me, yet again!

22

We had enough money to last for the next few weeks as once more we journeyed peacefully through Fenny Stratford, Bletchley, Wolverton and Blisworth. Outside Bletchley, we inspected an interesting house, set in large grounds surrounded by old stone ornaments. We explored the gardens but found no one to satisfy our curiosity as to its identity. On the way back to the boat, we decided to take a look around the churchyard where a large and rather ornate tombstone dedicated to an Italian attracted my attention. I wondered why he warranted such pomposity in this tiny rural churchyard. The vicar and his wife supplied the answer. During the last century the local wealthy squire had sent his eldest son on the Grand Tour. The young man returned not only with knowledge of the art treasures of Europe, but the great culinary skills of Italy – and he brought back an Italian chef for the Victorian mansion. The chef grew to love England and sent home for his fiancé. They married, had a family and their descendants are still in England today. The tombstone was erected in memory of that first chef by a grateful master.

Although we had now spent many months on the canals, we had yet to find anyone else living a similar life to ourselves. We'd met many people who worked and lived on their boats, but in every case so far they worked set areas only, and all had a base to which to return.

The only family living afloat, who worked the entire canal system, were Bob Bush, the canal painter and his father Binkie Bush, a ropemaker. We had encountered them on about three occasions since taking up our new life, and now as we approached Stoke Bruerne we met again. We rarely stopped to chat, but would call out as we passed each other, 'we're off to Birmingham', we would say. 'We're going to Tring,' Bob would reply.

Stoke Bruerne, is a popular canal village, probably the best known length of water in the country. Here the Waterways museum brings in the crowds. During the spring and summer you will usually find a party of school children buying one or other of the excellent books or souvenirs to be found in the shop alongside the splendid three-storey museum, which has been converted from a warehouse.

The Boat Inn, opposite, also attracts crowds who find it pleasant to sit outside with a drink and look at the terrace of canal cottages facing the pub. Sad to say, the brewers have modernised and extended the interior and spoilt the original local atmosphere. From Stoke Bruerne you can take a boat trip through Blisworth tunnel, all 3,000 yards of it and at 2 mph you can calculate how long you are in eerie darkness, broken only by the boat's front light and the daylight from five air vents, which also conduct water.

So be warned: be prepared for Blisworth Tunnel and wear protective wet weather gear always.

Whenever you leave a tunnel, no matter how long or short it is, the scene ahead as the pinhole of light increases in size is always fresh, clean and dazzling. And no more so than when you emerge from Blisworth tunnel when the grass, trees, and shrubs seem so much greener than ever before. The canal, turning smoothly past the village of Blisworth with its church perched on high by the side of the hill, presents one of the most beautiful of all waterside scenes.

And for us, it was a homecoming – *Bix*'s home at least. Blisworth was where she had been fitted out and where we had started our new life – almost a year previously. But what different people we were now. As we talked over our experiences with Peter Ellis, our boatbuilder, we could hardly realise that we were the same two oh-so-green canal boaters who had confidently waved him goodbye 12 months before.

We stayed at the boatyard a few days to have the engine checked and some painting done. What had the past 12 months brought to or taken from us? I wished I could have seen more of my family; it seemed strange not to meet up with one or other of them for months on end. And, of course, I would have loved to have kept the cats, although I had to admit that I rarely missed them now, in fact, I hardly thought about them at all.

Listening to live music had been a great part of our life until we took to the boat. Now we heard little live, but when we did, appreciated it all the more. Living without neighbours, without postman, milkman, dustman, in fact having no roots, had given us a sense of freedom with which came another experience. Owen and I drew closer together, closer than ever before. Often I found myself starting off a conversation in my head, and finishing it aloud, convinced in my happiness that Owen knew what was going on in my mind as surely as I.

We decided to spend the coming winter in the somewhat milder climate of Gloucester, where we could explore the Gloucester and Sharpness Canal. But first, another job awaited me, our youngest daughter Linda was about to produce baby number two and I was going to look after two-year-old Lewis for a week or so. As my own mother lived only 10 minutes away from Linda, I looked forward to spending many happy days with my family again. And the reunion was every bit as good as I'd hoped for.

Our second grand-daughter Tanis duly arrived, the days passing by quickly until I was on the train heading for Northampton and Owen. We had a glorious reunion too, with dinner in the Grand Hotel, and over this, Owen outlined the route to get us to Gloucester.

We would retrace our steps through Birmingham, to the Birmingham and Worcester Canal, out on to the River Severn, which would carry us to Gloucester.

I looked forward to the daily boat routine, until I remembered that this route entailed the Hatton flight of 21 locks. This time there would be no waiting for another boat to work through with us as it was now the first week in December and there would certainly be no hire boats or holidaymakers about in such raw, wintry weather.

We left early one bright cold day, with no one in sight, re-entering our special world, the one we had first encountered along this very stretch of water the previous year; a peaceful, silent world that belonged solely to us and the birds and animals.

23

The days seemed to pass all too quickly as we travelled through Braunston again and then continued along the Grand Union Canal towards Warwick and the Hatton Flight of locks. Once more, we were in that season of short days and long nights. Now we sat around the fire after our evening meal and out came the cards, the Scrabble and our well loved, well thumbed books. If life was cheaper aboard, it was certainly harder. When you must find your own water, dispose of your sewage and rubbish, day after day, and the temperature barely rises above freezing, then you cast your mind back to the days before those mundane tasks were yours. Whatever did you do with all that extra time?

Yet, here we were with extra chores and still time to enjoy in depth those wonderful sunsets; we needed no watch to tell us when it neared three o'clock because every winter afternoon we could see the V-formations of gulls wheeling high in the sky until all reported present and correct before setting off to their roost.

Through the Stockton Locks we were accompanied by a robin who would sit on the gate and stare at us inquisitively with his sharp eyes; then he would fly off suddenly, skimming low over the water and be waiting at the next lock. I had not realised before how much the robin loves water.

At night, after pulling down our glowing, orange blinds to give the boat a warm, cosy atmosphere, we could forget the icy winds that had chapped our faces during the day, and relax with a glow of satisfaction at our way of life.

After Royal Leamington Spa, the dreaded Hatton Flight awaited us and although it was a bitterly cold day for me at the tiller, Owen was soon sweating with the effort to work through such a formidable number of locks. But I was frozen and longed for a cup of hot coffee and a brief warm inside the boat.

At lock 12 we had to stop as a piece of rope fouled the propeller and poor Owen had to immerse his hands in the icy water for more than half an hour to free it. Despite this, we were clear of the locks by 2.30 and moored at Rowington, a tiny village with a population of 800; where they have hidden their post office and stores, I don't know. I walked up and down the only road they have and still couldn't find it.

The next morning, we left the Grand Union Canal a couple of miles past Rowington at the Kingswood Junction. Passing the entrance to the Stratford-on-Avon Canal we went on to join the Birmingham and Worcester Canal.

There followed three tunnels in a short stretch. The first is Kings Norton,

95

sometimes called West or Wast Hill tunnel. Before you enter this tunnel you are surrounded by depressing wasteland; 2,700 yards later you emerge into a fresh rural landscape.

We moored for lunch near the BWB yard at Tardebigge, with a glorious view of the lace-patterned spire of its church. We ate quickly, for ahead was the Tardebigge flight of locks. When I realised there were 30 to work, I wondered why most people talk only of Hatton ... maybe it's because the Tardebigge locks are narrow and the Hatton broad locks. The first lock, reputed to be the deepest in the system, is enough to put off anyone. As you slowly drop 14 feet the light grows murkier and the lock becomes quite eerie.

At lock 34 workmen were substituting hydraulic versions of the old paddle gear, so we had to wait awhile. Soon it began to darken and we realised we could not complete the flight before nightfall. Again, we found ourselves moored in a lock pound, but this time we had the blessing of the lock-keeper. Next morning, leakage had drained the pound in front of the next lock, so we had to wait until this was refilled before proceeding on our journey.

However, we had awoken to a beautiful morning, absolute silence, followed by a burst of song from the hungry fieldfares as they attacked the hedgerows. The canal was as still as if it had been in a picture. Then I realised that it was frozen with a thin coating of ice enough to give it a sheen.

As the day wore on, however, the temperature dropped and we found ourselves ice-breaking until evening. I had difficulty steering into some of the bottom locks because the nose of the boat nudged the sheets of ice on top of the frozen canal ahead, where they would break and jam the lock gates.

The Birmingham and Worcester canal from Tardebigge onwards is heavily locked and each day saw us absolutely worn out by dusk. Thankfully, we made Worcester on the Saturday before Christmas, in time to get a few bits and pieces for the weekend meals.

We knew Worcester, but only from the River Severn where we had moored, many years ago, just beyond the gracious cathedral's walls. From the canal, the city shows a very different face. Nothing lovely or gracious here, just a dreary derelict boundary to a shopping area. Even though they are developing a new housing estate alongside the water, they have given it an unbelievably ugly name. Surely the local council could have searched the archives for a more suitable name than The Blockhouse.

At Diglis Basin, the canal takes on an unrealistic coastal appearance thanks to the dozens of enormous ocean-going craft moored there. It comes as a shock after all those narrow locks to realise that from Diglis onwards the water caters for oil tankers and 1,000 ton merchantmen.

We had forgotten about this when we left the canal at Worcester and came out on to the Severn. Our plan was to go through Diglis Locks and on towards Tewkesbury, but the lock-keeper was unavailable; expecting no boats that day, he had gone off to do a spot of Christmas shopping.

Warwickshire canal scene near Napton

Swans fighting near Rugby on the North Oxford canal

Approaching a bridge near Brinklow, on the North Oxford Canal.

Easy mooring on Regents Canal and convenient for shopping around the Angel, Islington

The spectacular aqueduct on the Llangollen canal, 120 feet above the Dee Valley

As we could turn the boat anywhere on this wide river, we returned to Worcester and moored outside the Diglis Hotel for a 30th wedding anniversary dinner. On opening a card from my mother which contained a generous gift of money, I went straight to the Royal Worcester Porcelain works, next door to the hotel, and bought two Worcester coffee cups and saucers as a souvenir for us both.

We sat in the hotel lounge after a superb dinner, drinking an even more superb brandy. Quite the largest tabby cat I have ever seen was the only other occupant of this pleasant room. It was like sitting in our own home. Who would have thought, I wondered, to see us now, that we had enough money to keep us only for the next ten days or so. I mentioned this to Owen, as he settled comfortably into his armchair. 'For the first time in your life,' he said, 'you're getting your priorities right.'

The next day, we motored through Diglis Locks to find that the river grapevine had preceded us.

'Sorry about yesterday,' said the lock-keeper.

'No matter,' we told him, 'we've got plenty of time'. Recalling our bank balance, however, I didn't think ten days all that long.

The weather was unexpectedly windy and the river became quite choppy, the waves slapping so fiercely against the boat at times that they reached almost to the level of the windows. A new experience this, after navigating narrow canals. Another experience was lack of moorings. Mostly the river banks were very high making it impossible to get close to the shore to tie up. Our lunch stop that first day, after several unsuccessful attempts to get to the shore, was finally executed by my grabbing at the branch of an overhanging tree to which we tied up insecurely, leaving the back of the boat free. Not a good way to moor but we needed respite from the icy blasts that confronted us as we battled down river.

We remembered, from a previous holiday on the Severn, that Upton-on-Severn had a public mooring with wide steps leading to the river with rings attached for the boat ropes. So as we drew alongside, I had no hesitation in jumping off only to land in a squelch of oozy mud. The river had recently flooded leaving the steps covered in a glutinous layer of silt, quite unlike my memory of a summer mooring there.

The winds became gales during the night and the following day we found ourselves travelling unexpectedly fast as we were blown towards Tewkesbury. It was Christmas Eve and we decided to go through the lock at Tewkesbury and out on to the Avon, where we would stay for a couple of days over the Christmas period.

Once again, our plans were thwarted – this time because there was a BWB boat filled with tree trunks already in the lock. The lock-keeper informed us that it would probably stay there until after Christmas, as the tree-fellers who had brought it in had gone off for dinner, since when they had not been seen. So with the lock blocking us off from the Avon, we had to moor on the Severn. The usual moorings at Tewkesbury, just below the flour mills, were out of use thanks to some re-building being carried out on part of the mill.

We could find no other mooring and it was too late to attempt the remaining 15 miles to Gloucester. The lock-keeper obligingly allowed us to moor abreast of a large cruiser which was tied up adjoining his lock house.

It was a very quiet Christmas for us once more, but quite unlike last year's which, as our first, had an extra-special quality that I shall always treasure. I telephoned my mother, who was spending the day with one of our daughters, and she was the only person, apart from Owen, to whom I spoke throughout the day. On Boxing morning, we went along to what has become one of our favourite hotels, the Hop Pole Inn. In the past, we had eaten gloriously in their dining room, but now we could not afford such a luxury. Instead we treated ourselves to a brandy before walking along to Tewkesbury Abbey which seems much too large for such a small country town. I'm sure the parishioners who paid £450 for it in the sixteenth century were proud of it. What a ridiculous sum that seems in today's highly inflated market.

As if to compensate for the size of its church, Tewkesbury has some of the smallest and narrowest streets of any town. To be correct, they are alleys. There are dozens of them and, in fact, a map has been made of the alleys alone. Today, most are losing their neglected look and the properties abounding these areas are now eagerly sought after. There are, however, one or two near the river which still have a squalid Dickensian air about them.

We left Tewkesbury on Saturday morning hoping to get to Gloucester by the evening, but we only got as far as Upper Lode Lock, a mile from Tewkesbury as again we had surprised the lock-keeper. It is usual, apparently, for boats to inform lock-keepers of their destination who, after you have gone through one lock, inform the other lock-keepers to expect you. We had told the last lock-keeper that we were going to Tewkesbury and he had assumed that the boat would stay there. The River Severn, like the canals, had not met many boaters like us it seems.

We spent the day exploring the river banks. From the boating point of view, I found the river monotonous, the banks being so high that you see nothing of the surrounding countryside. Today we made up for it. The very flat water meadows around Upper and Lower Lode must have made the fighting even more hazardous when the last of the battles of the Wars of the Roses took place here ... the name of the area today is Bloody Meadow.

Next morning, the lock-keeper told us he had had the surprise of his life when he saw us moored outside his lock. He told us about the tidal part of the river which ran henceforward. The best place to moor, he said, was outside Gloucester Lock and, although he would let them know we were coming, we would have to ask the lock-keeper when he would pass us through. If any large cargo ships were in the Dock Basin, they would be attended to first.

Even with this prior knowledge, I was stunned by my first sight of the Gloucester and Sharpness Canal.

24

I don't know why I was so ill-prepared to see so much cargo being loaded
and unloaded in Gloucester docks. I'd read about them and the canal and
knew they catered for commercial shipping, but it wasn't until I saw these
merchantmen on the canal that I realised just how different life was going
to be whilst we explored this part of the inland waterway system.

As we gently rose out of the deep Gloucester Lock, I looked at two rather
bewildered faces peering down at me and the boat. We finally surfaced at
the top level and two men introduced themselves as Superintendent Watts
in charge of the docks and one of his assistants.

Mr Watts, very puzzled, wanted to know where we had come from.
Tewkesbury, we said. Where were we bound? The Gloucester and
Sharpness Canal.

'No,' he said, 'you can't, there's nowhere for you.' It was our turn to be
puzzled. Because of so much commercial craft, the BWB apparently did not
relish pleasure boats on the canal. There were no moorings, we were told,
no water, no gas, and no sanitary stations, except in the dock basin.

Our disappointment grew deeper, but we persisted in trying to persuade
Mr Watts that if only he would let us through the lock, we wouldn't mind
tying up in the dock basin for a few nights.

'The docks are locked at night – you can't sleep on board there.' I
explained how we were living on *Bix* permanently and travelling around
the 2,000 miles of the waterways and I also could now add, truthfully, that
we would be lecturing about the canals at a weekend course, in conjunction
with the publicity officer of the BWB later in the year, and naturally we
would like to have some pictures and stories about the Gloucester and
Sharpness Canal.

To digress a little, we had in fact been booked for this canal weekend as
an offshoot following a jazz weekend course for an adult education college.

Eventually Mr Watts relented and he pointed out a bridge crossing the
canal.

'Go under the bridge and tie up at Llanthony,' he said. 'You can stay 14
days.' After he had accepted our thanks and an invite for coffee in a day or
so, we all shook hands and *Bix* sailed out of the lock.

Whenever I think of a river, I visualise my part of the River Thames,
with its lighters, barges, cargo boats, cranes, derricks and the general hustle
of a working waterway. Mention the word canal and I'm in tranquil
waters, a snail in the hubbub of our frenetic civilisation.

These illusions were shattered as we sailed across Gloucester Docks,
passing several basins containing very large ships which were all in the

process of loading or unloading outside one of the many splendid warehouses surrounding the docks. Most of these lovely buildings are now protected properties and are safe therefore from the hands of the demolition squads.

As we approached the road bridge which crossed the boundary of the docks and canal, I heard a bell ring and noticed the bridge-keeper in an office by the side of the bridge. The traffic barriers were lowered and slowly the great bridge towered into the air and through we went – all that just for our little boat. I began to see why we hadn't been eagerly welcomed and I realised as we slid alongside the high stone wharf that this was in fact not just a canal but to give it its correct name the Gloucester and Sharpness Ship Canal.

On the smaller canals the iron rings to tie up the boat are about five inches diameter, but at Gloucester they measure about 15 inches diameter and are made of heavy iron, capable of holding a 1,000 tonner. They made our ropes look like string.

Once the boat was secure, I could see that I would have to be careful getting on and off it as the wharf was so much higher than the sides of the canals we were used to. To board the boat, I had to lean over until I could grasp hold of the top rail then, gingerly lowering one leg over the edge, I felt for the cat walk that protrudes round the boat. Once both feet were on this, I edged slowly along until I reached the back deck and was safe on board. In reverse, it was much harder, having to swing my legs up and over the high stone edge. From above poor *Bix* looked like a matchbox.

The wind was blowing onto the nose of *Bix*, so I decided to stay in the warmth and comfort and postpone my visit ashore to the next day.

Knowing that we were going to be in Gloucester for a while, we had written to Peter, a musician in Cheltenham. We hoped that he might be able to get Owen a few band jobs but we appreciated now how difficult work here would be if we could stay only 14 days.

About seven o'clock a knock on the door made me worry whether there had been second thoughts about our permit to stay. Owen opened the door and I heard a charming voice say, 'hallo, you won't know me, I'm Roger, a friend of Peter's. I play the piano.' An hour later, we were in Roger's comfortable house listening to a live music session between Owen, Roger and Peter, and Owen had been booked for two jobs the following weekend.

Things moved fast in Gloucester. Roger knew a committee member of a Canal Society close by who could help us find a mooring. He directed us to the nearest water standpipe and told us where we could order calor gas and have it delivered direct to the boat! After that, we decided two weeks were insufficient to explore Gloucester. We decided also to seek work the very next day.

Our mooring at Llanthony Wharf was situated some seven minutes from the city itself and next morning we found that the job centre was almost the first place in Southgate. Gloucester is beautifully and simply laid out with four main streets – Northgate, Eastgate, Southgate, Westgate – meeting at the centre of a cross, naturally called The Cross.

There were dozens of jobs available and in less than half an hour, I had an appointment that afternoon for eight weeks' work as a merchandiser for a bakery, part-time, three days a week. By four o'clock that first day, I had the job and rushed back to tell Owen, who was starting work on Monday – as a clerk in an office in the centre of Gloucester.

We behaved like a couple of kids, dancing up and down the boat. We sat in front of the fire and had a glass of sherry. Was it ridiculous for two middle-aged people to celebrate getting work on their first day in a new place when they had no idea where their home would be in a week or so's time? We didn't think so.

We saw in 1976 with Peter who stayed overnight. The next day, we set off on our first trip down the Gloucester and Sharpness. After a mile we reached Hemstead Bridge, where the towpath was more like those we were used to and we asked if it was possible to moor overnight. The bridgekeeper saw no objection, and although we went back to Llanthony Wharf that day, we knew now that we had at least one more place to tie up.

And that's how we found it throughout the whole canal. Every few days, we moved up and down and found the bridgekeepers wonderful people. We exchanged bottles of home-made wine with two of them, another told us to make use of his outdoor lavatory whenever we liked. We found a water supply, the calor gas was delivered regularly to the boat once a week, and, believe it or not, the postman actually delivered a letter to the boat addressed, 'on the Gloucester and Sharpness Canal.' It was from a canal enthusiast living locally who had seen us pass and who wrote to say we could moor near his house any night we chose. Marvellous people – marvellous canal.

The New Year started with gale force winds throughout England with the south west getting the worst of it – especially just outside Gloucester and around Evesham. So much for our coming to a milder climate. After a noisy night, when the boat was viciously blown against the stone-sided wharf, we rose early to start our respective jobs.

I was shown the shops and stores where I would be working and, to my delight, was given a Bedford van of my own to get me to and from the towns around Gloucester which I would be covering. I had to learn to call some of the products by different names: what I had known as bread rolls in Kent were now called cobs or batches; what I had called a sandwich loaf was now a brick, not a tempting name I thought for bread.

By the end of our first week in Gloucester, Owen had been booked for three band jobs a week and we were all set for an exciting few weeks in our new home-town.

25

Each week we moored in a different location, sometimes at Hemstead Bridge, or Sellars Bridge, and then we would return to Llanthony Wharf on Sunday afternoon to be ready for work again.

Our jobs had hours that could be re-arranged easily so we managed to take four days off following a weekend which enabled us to reach Sharpness. We had a glorious trip – a honeymoon one.

In the last band Owen had put together before we moved from the farm, he recruited a marvellous girl pianist, Rosemary. Rosemary then married David who occasionally played the double bass in Owen's band, and to whose wedding we were invited. I even bought myself a new blouse, the first new clothing purchased since coming to *Bix*. Our standard of living did not allow us to splash on the kind of wedding present we would have liked, but I suddenly thought that what we *did* have and *could* offer was a honeymoon boat trip.

David and Rosemary eagerly accepted our invitation so the four of us returned to Gloucester to start off early the next morning on a joint honeymoon.

David had been aboard *Bix* for a couple of days during the autumn, but for Rosemary it was not only her first view of *Bix*, but also her first boating experience. Once she had found the best way to board the boat, (like me she found it difficult when we were moored against high stone wharves) she became really enthusiastic.

The first bridge, Hemstead, opened for us and we waved to our bridgekeeper friend as we sailed through. We told him we would be going as far as Frampton on Severn, to which he nodded, meaning that he would let the other bridgekeepers know. The next three bridges have greater headroom and do not have to be opened for us, but the keepers usually look out to give us a wave.

After Hemstead, the industrial estates start to thin out. Once past the gas works, there is only the slaughter-house by the side of Sims Bridge and then, thankfully, you are in wide, flat countryside again. Happily today, there were no poor animals waiting in cattle trucks to be sent squealing to their deaths; and they do scream as I'd heard many a time when moored at Hemstead.

The canal soon runs parallel to the River Severn; and at Rea Bridge, we tied up and walked a few hundred yards to the place where people watch the famous Severn Bore. The bridgekeeper here had a tide timetable and told us the best days to view the highest of these. We made a note to return in March to film this incredible quirk of nature, when the tide from Bristol meets the tide coming down the Severn. For a few moments, the River Severn stops flowing in any direction, then the oncoming tide takes over and a wall of water streams up river.

After coffee, we continued through desolate meadows, but if you turn around and look back towards Gloucester, you get the best view of the large hill which lies just on the edge of town at Tuffley. This is Robins Hill Wood, once the boundary of the land held by the wealthy Llanthony Friary, the remains of which can be seen by the side of the canal at Llanthony wharf, near the entrance to the docks.

At Sellars Bridge, the skyline is broken by oil storage tanks which mark the furthest point up canal that the tankers can come. By this time, we were accustomed to seeing the large oil tankers, and we knew *Bude* and *Bisley* by sight as well as the local hire cruisers. Another vessel we saw quite often was *Torbay*, as she moored opposite us in Gloucester. She brought from Northern France and Belgium a cargo of grey stones, all numbered or marked and unloaded into piles on the wharf opposite our mooring, for use in repairs to Gloucester Cathedral. The original Cotswold stone is either unavailable or what there is doesn't match as well as that from across the Channel.

A couple of miles past Sellars Bridge brought us to Saul Junction where the Stroudwater Canal joins the Gloucester and Sharpness. At present, the Stroudwater is unnavigable, until the strenuous efforts of a flourishing canal restoration society bear fruit.

Saul Junction is the only place on the Gloucester and Sharpness where one can get a nostalgic whiff of canal life as led elsewhere on the system. There are many moorings for pleasure boats and also one or two working boats can be seen tied up there.

We decided to moor the night at Frampton on Severn, just past Cadbury's milk powder depot. The factory and wharf are beautifully kept, most of the paintwork a deep olive green, which almost matched the Danish boat that brought a cargo of dried milk while we were tied up that night.

As the wash from this vessel tore along the canal, it was easy to see why we had had to extend our mooring ropes to reach the bollards cemented at intervals on the far side of the towpath. Whilst moored with our own mooring spikes at Hemstead one day, they had been torn out of the ground with the force of a similar wash and we had been cast adrift. It was then that we learned to lengthen our ropes to reach the bollards. Photographs of *Bix* taken alongside these 1,000 tonners show her looking like the proverbial match box tossing along in their wash.

Frampton on Severn is attractive, especially the village green which, although not wide, stretches out to match the village itself and continues for about half a mile along the road. The next day brought us to the highlight of the trip – at Patch Bridge, by the side of the lovely named Shepherds Patch, we tied up and headed towards the Slimbridge Wildfowl Trust. Even before we reached the entrance we had stopped at least half a dozen times to examine a species of duck unknown to us.

We'd chosen the right day, a bright, sunny January morning, not too cold but crisp and dry. We'd kept this part of the journey a secret from the honeymooners and Rosemary especially was delighted with our surprise.

There were few other visitors to the Park and we had it very much to ourselves. We took dozens of photos and Owen was so fascinated by the flamingos that he used almost a whole reel of film on them. We stayed for an excellent lunch in the restaurant and even there thanks to its picture windows, we could continue our observations. We spent well over three hours at Slimbridge which wasn't long enough. However, we wanted to reach Purton that night where we had been recommended to 'a real old pub, which sells the strong stuff.' The 'strong stuff' didn't interest us so much as none of us is a beer drinker, but we were all interested in old buildings.

We moored for the night past the two swing bridges there and about a hundred yards from the pub which we visited after dinner. A long passage led to a tiny bar beyond which lay a vast room packed with bottles, crates, glasses and lord knows what else. An elderly lady was serving two customers standing in front of the little bar and blocking it completely. There were no chairs or tables, or even room for them, in this narrow passageway.

A list of drinks pinned to the wall advertised 'Lunatic Broth'. That must be the strong stuff, we decided. David and I opted for this, while Owen and Rosemary stuck to their usual. After we had been served, we were told that the doors on either side of the passage led to the bars so we took our drinks and tried the first: only to be greeted by a blaring juke box. We tried the other room which we had to ourselves – for the next 40 minutes or so. Apart from an old dark settle against one wall, the rest of the furniture was as motley a collection as you would find in any roadside cafe or beach hut.

Lunatic Broth turned out to be a poor quality barley wine, so our evening out proved a disappointment. Maybe we had been spoilt, living for 20 years in a part of Kent that boasts real village inns that provide good food and drink as well as interesting conversation with the locals.

We decided that a glass of home-made hawthorn wine and a game of Scrabble on *Bix* would suit us better and that's exactly what we did.

We completed the rest of the journey to Sharpness by lunch time next day. Here a boatyard was open at the end of the arm, jutting off the canal, just before it enters Sharpness docks and we sailed in to top up our diesel. Although there were many pleasure boats moored along the arm, the yard owner was surprised to see us. He asked, somewhat incredulously, if we were winter cruising. When we explained that we lived on board permanently he was speechless, and when we went on to say that we were all on honeymoon, that gave him as good a story as he'll ever tell I should think.

The Sharpness docks cater for large shipping from all over Europe but with only one large ship lying alongside a wharf, it did not seem overstretched to us.

Our time was running out and so we turned back for Gloucester. At

Purton that night we photographed the wrecks of boats that have been used to shore up the sides of the River Severn. Sad to see the lines of wooden ribs jutting out of the mud and concrete, a kind of boat cemetry I suppose you'd call it.

Back once again in Gloucester, it was time to say goodbye to the honeymooners. How fast the days had flown, but what good times we had all had.

After David and Rosemary had left, Owen posed a startling question, 'what do you think of advertising for paying guests?' He went on, 'they could have our bedroom, as Dave and Rose did, and we could sleep on the bed settee in the lounge. It seemed to work last week.' I had to admit it had, but then we knew Dave and Rose. What would it be like with strangers at such close quarters?

We discussed the idea with a few people. Hotel boats, yes, but paying guests living as family, that they had not seen, and on a narrow boat!

Still, I enjoyed cooking, we both loved entertaining and we certainly liked meeting people so we decided to put an advertisement in a Sunday newspaper and sit back to see what would happen next.

26

Our stay in Gloucester was the most static part of our boating life so far. I appreciated to the full that we could arrange regular social events and hear and participate in live music again. We made friends with the BWB boatmen as they regularly passed with their loaded barges, and we even had a French corvette as a neighbour for three days when it paid a courtesy visit to the city.

During the latter part of February, on my way to work, wherever the boat was moored I saw men on bicycles carrying strange-looking fishing nets, long handles with a triangular shaped fine mesh net, or scoop at the end. They were after elvers, the baby eels that arrive in the River Severn during the late winter and early spring after a journey of several thousands of miles across the oceans from the Sargasso sea. It seemed so unfair, after such an ordeal, to finish up in a pan of hot bacon fat as someone's special breakfast dish. But these white wiggly wormlike creatures are a rare delicacy not only in England but in France and Poland too.

A boat astern of us at Llanthony wharf contained two large water tanks into which the owners tipped elvers each day. They planned to cross the Channel and sell their catch. Owen wanted to try some for himself, but for once I was not attracted to the local delicacy ... and at 75p a pound, I thought them expensive. However, we became friendly with the fishermen and we thought that maybe they would let us have a few at a cheap rate before they set sail. Unfortunately for us, and for the boat owners, one of their tanks sprang a leak and they lost a great deal of their catch. They were now, in fact, advertising for live elvers hoping that they would get enough from the individual fishermen to enable them to carry out their original plan to sell in France. I couldn't help wondering if the escapees would survive and breed in the canal or would the water be too polluted for them to live that long.

We made many new friends in Gloucester, what with Owen playing regularly and, of course, both of us working. If we hadn't kept moving the boat, up and down the canal, life would have become almost normal once again!

Gloucester had obviously gone through a recent bout of redevelopment and lost its sleepy country town look. Now it boasted the best planned enclosed shopping precinct I'd ever seen and what was more, it was appreciated by the shoppers, for not once did I see toffee papers, cigarette packets, or lolly sticks thrown carelessly on to the ground. Whether on a Monday morning or busy Friday night, the precinct always bore a welcoming, clean face. Plenty of seats dotted about gave it a clublike atmosphere, where the elderly took advantage of resting and the young used it as a meeting place.

'Under the clock' was a favourite, but it was difficult to find a friend if the time was approaching the hour as all the world rendezvoused then. It is erected high on the wall above the entrance to the market, where incidentally you can buy lovely Gloucester and Cotswold farm cheeses, butter, home made bread and vegetables. On the hour small hammers strike the bells to play nursery rhymes and folk tunes. At the same time emerges a parade of wooden figures representing a band. Children and adults stand and stare daily ... I always stopped to watch, and before we left Gloucester I was to enjoy the spectacle even more when I showed it to my three-year-old grandson, Lewis.

As happy as we were, we both knew, however, that it was time for us to move on again. Mr Watts, the superintendent, had been more than helpful to us in allowing us to stay and I now had plenty of film, and with the help of the splendid City Reference Library, information to make up my lecture.

We started making plans on where to go and when. After poring over our maps we decided to head for Birmingham and then the north western canals. First, however, we had to see the famous Severn bore, but I had an even more important task ... to find a chiropodist. My feet were painful and if anything proved that life had changed for me, it was that. Once upon a time, my life ran with almost clockwork precision. Twice yearly appointments with dentist and chiropodist were regularly made and kept. Now, here I was waiting until my feet hurt before even bothering to look for a chiropodist.

Gloucester, however, had three in the City centre and the second one I tried gave me a booking within the week. It was bliss to have my feet cossetted again, and I chatted on about how impressed I was with Gloucester. The chiropodist seemed pleased and interested to hear about my boating life. I enthused, especially over the replanning, and said how much I loved the way they had still retained the route of the old city wall on the present day street names. And, how pleasing, also, to see the remains of the old Friary left standing, adjoining the walls of the new precinct. He explained how difficult it had been for the city to make the choice between standing still or re-planning. He obviously loved Gloucester and knew a great deal about its transformation. I mentioned this and he replied, 'I was mayor at the time' ... with his scalpel in one hand and my foot in the other how glad I was that I had approved of his new city.

To see the Severn bore we moved down the canal and moored, just past the Rea bridge where we confirmed the times of the next three bores. With us were our daughter Linda and her husband and three-year-old Lewis. Owen and I went down at 10 o'clock that pitch black night. We stood alone on the high river bank, piercing the inky night with our torch. The river ran smoothly downstream while we waited, growing colder and colder. Then in the distance came a roar, like wind through a tunnel, which grew quickly louder. We directed our light downstream to the bend of the river and there it was, a huge wall of water roaring and tearing its way up the banks, pulling aside saplings and branches, beating and smothering reeds, and grasses. As it swirled past us, now almost at our feet, we could see the river had risen about five feet, and then it was away on up river leaving only the heavy, grey waters of the now swollen Severn.

On our way home we spotted another torch bobbing about on the lawn of a house. A man and woman were bending over the grass.

'Have you lost something?' we asked.

'No,' came the reply. 'We're picking up elvers – the bore always throws them on to the lawn ... they'll make a good breakfast.' How easy it is for some people to catch elvers!

We all captured the bore on film next morning. I expected hundreds of people at Stonebench, reckoned to be the best spot to see the bore, but there were no more than about 40 people. Later on, we were given, as a farewell present by Owen's boss, a book on the Severn bore. On the flyleaf, he had written, 'just a small reminder of a local "non-event" '. We thought it terrific, especially at night, but that's not how the locals see it.

We had three farewell parties ... with musicians, business friends, and a lovely morning coffee one with the artistic bridgekeeper at Sellars Bridge. I had longed to enter a bridgekeeper's cottage. Each canal has its own style of architecture; the Gloucester and Sharpness cottages are single-storied with two doric columns and a canopy roof in front, giving them a classical facade. They add a great deal of charm to this rather austere canal.

At Sellars Bridge, my dream came true. We were invited inside the cottage and, what was more, shown the bridgekeeper's collection of beloved Spode birds. What sacrifices he must have made to save for them, but then he was a true artist. One only had to look in the fireplace to see that. In the corner, by the grate, stood a dolphin, made of wood, with a roguish glass eye winking at you and poised ready to dive – a beautiful thing. Our friend chuckled when I bent down to pick it up. 'I found that bit of driftwood a few weeks ago, have a look.' He handed it over. 'I put a marble in that groove, and there, I had my dolphin.' He smiled as he replaced it. Happy man!

On saying goodbye to Owen's boss who had gladly allowed Owen to re-arrange his work to fit in with band jobs he gave us yet another book. This was the story of Gloucester, with beautiful photographs to bring back happy memories of our stay on the local canal.

27

We saw the first of the year's hire boats at Upton on our way back along the Severn. It had come from a yard at Worcester which was our next pick up point for mail. And this was doubly important now because, incredibly, we had had eight replies about the paying guests idea of whom at least one couple were definitely booking a holiday.

Our offer to lecture had also brought encouraging results and a weekend course at Theobalds Park college was the first one of the new courses that we would be running in two week's time.

What with planning lectures, offering articles to hard-to-please editors, and of course moving the boat continuously, we had retraced our journey up the Severn and I was shopping again in Worcester before I'd had time for the river scenery to pall. It was still, however, bitterly cold. Forever in my mind's eye, I associate icy winds with Gloucester and the River Severn ... never have I felt so cold as during those winter months.

The post was all we could have wished. Our couple had booked for Easter weekend, Saturday to Tuesday morning. What had we done? Suppose we didn't like them or they us! You can find few places in a narrow boat to get away from each other. Suppose they didn't like my cooking ... anyway too late now, they were just three weeks away.

In the mail was also the splendid news that a woman's magazine had accepted one of my articles at a fee we could live off for almost a month, and they were asking for photos of the boat and me! That one acceptance made me forget about the many, many rejection slips that I had had for a while.

We left the Severn at Stourport and navigated the various locks and basins which lead on to the Staffs and Worcester canal. Stourport has a special place in our hearts, for it was here during the 1960's that we first discovered canals. We were boating on the Avon and Severn that year and had moored at Stourport one afternoon. Fascinated by the town, we wandered around, and saw boats apparently moving at the bottom of a narrow street. We approached and found ourselves looking into a lock. Not only were there boats below us, but boats almost above us, as the various levels of canals, basins and locks converge at this Clapham Junction of the canal system. From then on we were hooked on canals. Now, ten years later, we were back again, this time working through with not only our own boat but our home as well.

After lunch we had a successful shopping expedition and each bought a pair of boating trousers from the local Oxfam shop. I am a great enthusiast for Oxfam shops and give and buy at any opportunity.

It was with mixed feelings that we rejoined the narrow canal system for although I prefer it to the wide commercial Gloucester and Sharpness, we immediately encountered one of its disadvantages, and were jammed in the entrance of the very first lock by a plank of wood. It's not too bad if this happens in fine weather and there are other boaters around to help, but it's far from welcome when it's windy and raining as it was that day. However, it's a bit like having a baby, I think. Once the worst is over, you relax and enjoy the good bit to such an extent that the bad bit is forgotten ... until the next time.

We soon hit one of the good bits as the Stafford and Worcester became rural and tranquil and kept us on the lookout to see the first of the immigrant birds arrive. Alas, the industrial fringes of Kidderminster appeared and we found ourselves manoeuvring between the high walls of carpet factories, and warehouses, then under two low bridges, both dark and gloomy. Beyond it we found a brighter mooring by the church.

Kidderminster is well known for carpets but not so well known as the birthplace of that pioneer of the Post Office, Rowland Hill. The town has a statue of its well known son, outside the Post Office, of course. You may have trouble finding it today, for what the town council did not foresee was that the Post Office would be moved! So don't go to the glass and concrete monstrosity in the new shopping precinct, instead seek out the lovely building at the other end of the town, the old Post Office. You can't miss it — there's a statue of Rowland Hill outside!

Our peaceful mooring outside the church wasn't ... take warning and listen to the church bells before tying up for the night. This one had what must be the loudest in the country, faithfully proclaiming each hour through the night.

The canal is beautiful from here onwards and we sailed along smooth waters with fresh sprigs of grass and reeds bursting out along the banks. At bridge 28 we passed a pub dating back to 1300 which is said to be the home of Dick Whittington's grandfather; and its name of course is Whittington.

Next came the curiously named wharf of Stewpony and a pub with the same name. I can find no trace of the history of this unusual name. Certainly, the nearby castle has nothing to do with it. Stourton Castle is a jumble of architectural design, starting about the 15th century. It looks as if every succeeding generation has had a go at an extension. It is the birthplace of Cardinal Pole, who became Archbishop of Canterbury, after Cranmer.

Not far past Stewpony is the junction of the Stourbridge Canal with the Stafford and Worcester, Stourton Junction. Here we took the right hand branch and were faced immediately with the 16 Stourbridge locks. The locks could be used only at certain times because of a water shortage but we were lucky to have the help of the lock-keeper to see us through.

Another canal junction appears on the scene after the locks. This is Leys Junction, where the Dudley Canal joins the Stourbridge and this was our next stretch of water. We were really in the heart of heavy industry now and during the next few days the scenery grew more and more depressing, the water like slimy indian ink. We moored for the night at Brierley Hill at the bottom of the Delph locks where our windows on one side looked out on a massive tower-block estate. The other side faced a moonscape of grey slate desert, so vast that the earth-moving machines working there looked like model toys. One day that greyish mass will be transformed into a green and open park and recreation ground, five years hence.

As with so many industrial canals, access to the town is difficult. Usually it's a case of walking along until you espy a hole in the fence or an alley between factory walls. I'm glad we found our way out to Brierly Hill, once a famous name in the glass industry.

We climbed a steep road leading to the church as the sun was setting. From the churchyard, spread out before us were hundreds of roof tops, chimneys, and flat factory sheds, almost on a level with our feet ... bathed in a dusky rose pink as the rays from the setting sun pierced the cloud of smoke hanging above them as if held on fine threads.

Next morning, we had proof that the holiday season had started, even here in this industrial zone. We had just entered the first of the Delph locks when an American took our photo. The previous summer, we had been snapped, clicked and shuttered at every day on the Oxford and Regent Canal, mostly by Americans. I had not expected to find any tourists along this polluted stretch of water, but there he was clicking, oohing and aahing and smiling his thanks.

When I offered him a trip to the next lock, all of 20 yards, he leapt aboard immediately and proceeded to use up about two reels of film on Owen opening the lock, shutting the lock, the interior of the lock and then with a dive, the interior of the boat!

His friend remained on the towpath, much amused by his antics. No wonder. He lived about 200 yards from the locks, in one of the tower blocks. Born in a canal house since pulled down he could remember working boats plying up and down the canal. Now he had had his fill, felt nothing for them and would not have been on the towpath today if it hadn't been that his American brother-in-law, on holiday over here, had noticed our boat travelling 'along that ditch.'

Our native friend agreed with us that it must have been about twenty years since this canal had been dredged, and soon we discovered how right we all were. Halfway up the eight Delph locks, we ran out of water. Later still found us untangling plastic bags, wire and rope from the propeller. One factory followed another and at one time we seemed to breathe unadulterated sulphur fumes. I had had more than enough of boating by the time we moored that day, near Pudding Green Junction.

After several attempts to tie up we spotted another boat moored and secured in front of her. Our far from salubrious surroundings included a huge steam hammer that deafened us throughout the night ... what wouldn't I have given for the Kidderminster church bells!

Within minutes of tying up, our neighbour started to burn some old rubber tyres on the towpath. As it turned out he was a well-known character on this part of the canal, born on a working boat and had spent all his life on them. He was still at work, carting rubbish from the centre of

Birmingham. He had little time to talk as he was busy sorting his rubbish, but we have met and helped each other through many a Birmingham canal since and he's a grand old man indeed. I just wish he hadn't started burning those tyres at the end of such a trying day.

Our main destination was Gas Street Basin, in the heart of Birmingham itself, once a thriving business centre for the working boats on the system. Today, many of the old boats are converted into houseboats, a sight that draws many tourists to this part of Birmingham. Alas, however, in 1976 Gas Street Basin fell victim to the demon demolitioner ... by a mistake I was told of the City Council. Lack of communication, the cause of so many wars, started things going wrong between the city departments which led to all the listed buildings being pulled down. Today when you visit Gas Street Basin, you'll see, beyond the boats, a desert of brick and rubble, at the back entrance of ATV's TV Centre, plus other towering concrete slabs that laughingly go by the name of a City Centre.

I wasn't sorry to leave Birmingham after a couple of days and even the black slime on the gates of the first lock on the Wolverhampton level failed to persuade me to return. When the water changed to a pale green sludge, however, I had second thoughts for it was the most repulsive we had yet encountered, caused, no doubt, by waste from an adjoining chemical works. That greeny slime accompanied us until we moored near Dudley zoo.

There followed another day of steel works with furnaces spitting only yards from the towpath, vast cranes lifting iron to sites where even vaster hammers smashed and flattened it, to be collected by magnet and dumped in the hungry bellies of more furnaces. All day long, heat, noise, dirt ... I'd read about these places and now I saw them I wondered again how man could stay sane in such an environment.

We reached Wolverhampton by the late afternoon and found a convenient mooring with excellent access to the town. As strangers we made for the local information bureau and were directed to the town hall where a kind and efficient commissionaire gave us a splendid copy of the town guide – for free. One up to Wolverhampton!

We shopped in the new precinct, excellent cheese from Woolworths, and to my delight, discovered a theatre where we immediately booked seats for the evening performance. How I enjoyed my first live theatre after so many months. It was an excellent production of an Alan Aykbourn play, but sparsely attended. I was told that the house was full on most weekends but without a national celebrity, comedian or pop singer, the locals abandon the theatre mid-week. It was sad to see the rows of empty seats in such a well maintained old building with its elaborate plaster decor, its tower proscenium arch, lovely pastorally painted safety curtain ... the only sign of updating is staggered seating, a sensible decision. However, we thoroughly enjoyed our evening, and how convenient for boaters. Where else, I wonder, could you enjoy a live theatre performance, pop into a nearby hotel for a drink after, and be home in bed twenty minutes after curtains?

Owen wrote to the Council thanking them for their well-written guide and congratulating them on their theatre which they acknowledged warmly. We'll return.

It was time to collect our first paying guests, so we headed for the more rural waters of Autherley junction which, although only some four miles from Wolverhampton, involves 21 locks. We thought we would give ourselves a day to recover and prepare the boat for yet another new venture in our lives.

28

Our guests had arranged to arrive about two o'clock, but we noticed a car by the canal at midday. We ignored it as there were four people inside and I carried on with the final touches to the bedroom, while Owen prepared a salad lunch. Then a man and woman left the car and approached the boat, calling our name. It was THEM. I stopped shaking the rugs and, shaking myself, explained that the bedroom wasn't quite ready.

'We're early, I know, but I'm that keen to get going,' the blonde curls shook as Florence laughed away my nervous excuses.

Jack, obviously resigned to his wife's enthusiasm, smiled and told us to carry on; they were going to have sandwiches in the car with their two sons, who had brought them to the boat. I made them a pot of tea, and inside the boat listened to their excited chatter from the car whilst we gulped a hasty lunch ourselves.

Florence had said in her letter that she would like to cruise along the Shropshire Union canal, but when she discovered there were more locks and that they were nearer to us if we went along the Stafford and Worcester, then that was where she decided to go.

My worries about paying guests disappeared for we got on famously. In fact, I seemed to be on holiday too, responsible only for the domestic side of the trip. Owen steered while Florence and Jack took over the lock work which they loved. They even moored us under Owen's supervision.

Florence learned to steer but Jack was happy to stand and stare, thoroughly relaxed. We had excellent weather, quite hot for April and travelled more miles per day than Owen and I ever managed on our own. As it was Easter weekend quite a few boats accompanied us through Penkridge and on towards Great Haywood where the Stafford and Worcester joins the Trent and Mersey. Beautiful countryside greeted us all the way, the hedgerows in full leaf and the birds in full song, including the pheasant which seems plentiful around the Coven area.

Penkridge is the first village within easy reach of the canal, but a main road cutting through the village disturbs any peace it may have once had. Five miles on is Weeping Cross, once a famous canal junction but the traffic thunders over Bridge 98 to spoil this too. Stafford, however, is less than ten minutes away by bus, making this a convenient mooring place for restocking food cupboards. We gave the town a miss this time as we had planned to moor at an unusual part of the canal that night. Tixall Wide is wide, the canal resembling a huge lake as it spreads its waters to lap the edge of what was once the parkland of Tixall Hall.

All that remains of the hall is the gatehouse standing like an elaborate sore thumb amongst farmland. Each time I pass this spot I have the same thought: if that four-storied structure was only the gatehouse, what size was the actual hall? Obviously, the family was wealthy and influential, too, for they refused to allow the canal company to cut through this spot unless they made the canal wide enough to look like a lake when seen from the house.

As a result of this somewhat excessive demand, a spread of reeds curves round the edge of this bulge in the canal and provides excellent breeding facilities for wildlife. Whatever time of year or day you will see someone staring through binoculars across Tixall Wide. So we are the lucky ones after all.

It was here that I saw my first crested grebes and I hoped in turn to show these rather shy birds to Florence. You have to be quick to spot them for they dive below the surface the moment they spot you and re-emerge only when in the camouflage of the reeds. We were lucky and I enjoyed watching the pleasure in Florence's face as I pointed them out. Jack was too late, but there were plenty of coots, moorhens, lapwings, kingfishers, sparrow hawks and masses of finches ready to flaunt their colour and song before us. The coots as usual squabbled and behaved as if the Wide should belong exclusively to them.

During this disturbance, the delicate fawny-feathered grebe, with its reed-stalk neck, glides and dives unconcernedly, now and again surprising the watcher as one grebe dives and two surface!

We had reached Tixall Wide on Sunday night and I thought Florence seemed rather quiet after dinner. I suppose it was because tomorrow was their last day and I was right, but I was also surprised when she said, 'would it be all right if we ... I mean ... well, can we stay until Thursday, we're having such a wonderful time?'

Owen and I were overjoyed and, of course, we said yes.

Later that evening Jack telephoned his son and puzzled him with the news that he was not to pick them up as planned, and that he would ring again on Thursday morning.

The Trent and Mersey canal joins the Stafford and Worcester at Great Haywood, which is less than a mile from Tixall Wide. It was a canal we knew quite well, having cruised it the previous winter. I knew I could stock up with food to meet this unexpected development at Rugeley, which was the first place of any size that we would pass ... and that was only a few miles from the junction.

With the extra time, it was possible to show our guests around the grounds of Shugborough Hall, the home of the Earl of Lichfield. This magnificent house stands close to the River Sow which itself runs very near to the canal. The grounds contain several monuments and small temples, some with odd names like Tower of the Winds.

The house belongs to the National Trust. On a previous visit, we had been puzzled by an early picture of the house and river, as if one had been painted the wrong way round. As we stared towards the river, our guide explained that the picture showed the original position of the river in the

17th century. One day the owner decided that he would prefer to see it from a favourite room in the opposite side of the house. To get his way most of the village had to be destroyed, and the course of the river was redirected. The villagers were moved to new cottages, still standing incidentally in a lane in what is now Great Haywood.

Florence and Jack decided that there was time only to explore the grounds. Jack, I know, would have been interested in some of the exhibits in the Museum of Stafford life which is housed in the stables, but for them the boat came first.

We continued down the Trent and Mersey towards Colwich Lock, where I looked forward to meeting Val and Terry again. This turned out to be the highlight of the holiday, as not many people get to see the inside of a lock cottage. Florence and Jack not only did just that but when they discovered that Terry was a solo whist fanatic like themselves, they stayed up playing cards until two in the morning with Owen as the fourth player. I sat in front of a roaring fire in the next room with Val, hearing about an adventurous American holiday. Val had had a wonderful time, but nothing she had seen compared with life in her lock cottage.

Next morning, as I looked towards Cannock Chase, I couldn't help agreeing with her, but if only the wretched railway company hadn't built so close to the canal, it would have been paradise.

Val presented me with a pot of geraniums to stand atop the boat. The gardening urge was upon me again this spring. Lettuce seeds were emerging from margarine tubs, and the flaunting red flowers showed up well against the light green lettuce leaves ... a real roof garden.

Enthusiastic Florence, on being told that the Coventry canal joined the Trent and Mersey at Fradley junction, asked if we could cruise along it and so after shopping in Rugely, a depressing place, we continued our journey through decrepit canal country until we reached the modern coal mine just outside the town; flanked by smart lawns and flower beds, it belies all pictures of coal mines I've ever seen.

The next place is Armitage which is dominated by a factory making sinks, baths, lavatory pans, all bearing the name of the village. Which came first the village or the factory? On the wall of the factory facing the canal neon letters report the distance to London and Scotland. As this hardly interests the canal traveller, I think it must be for the benefit of railway passengers on the opposite side.

The only peaceful spot here is Spode House. High on a brow with sweeping lawns to the canal and adjacent to the imposing Hawkesyard Priory, Spode House was originally Armitage Park. Its connection with the Spode family dates from 1839 when widow Mary Spode moved from Great Fenton in the potteries with son Josiah, then 16 years old. Josiah spent the rest of his life at Spode House and died in 1893 leaving the property to a Dominican order who are still in possession. Today it is used as a centre for adult education courses. Due to subsidence caused by coal mining, Spode House has already dropped some three feet. Let's hope the National Coal Board find a solution to this problem before we lose another part of our heritage.

Handsacre sees the last of the rubbish covered canal side, and before reaching Fradley junction you cruise through silver birches of Ravenshaw Woods.

A pretty lock house at Middle Lock is the last before running right into the Coventry canal where our destination was Tamworth, some 15 miles away, the pick-up point for Jack and Florence. There was no time to explore Whittington or Hopwas for boating was what our guests had come for and still wanted. This was different from our normal life, when we had time to stop whenever we felt inclined. Owen and I had travelled the Coventry canal several times before but I made a note, however, of the large dandelions growing in Hopwas woods ... they would make lovely wine.

We turned into the Birmingham and Fazeley canal for a few yards, so that Florence could boast she had been on four canals and resumed our course to Tamworth.

It was lunch for five at Tamworth as we included Robert. Florence and Jack told their son all about the holiday throughout the meal and Robert wished that he too had been with us. I thought that pretty encouraging coming from a sailor on leave from the Royal Navy.

We said goodbye to two people who were now more than guests. I hope they realised how much we'd enjoyed their company. I learned a lot from Jack, a Sheffield steel-worker working to a background of noise and confusion ... a quiet man whose sincerity and goodness showed in his approach to life. Florence was the perfect foil to such a man – loving, gay, energetic, always bubbling over, off to do something new, something exciting.

A week later, we received a poem from them in thanks for their holiday. What a wonderful start to our paying guest adventure.

29

Life resumed its slow tempo as we turned for the Hopwas woods and the dandelions. They grew abundantly and I was soon making my way along the towpath bent double intent on picking that large one over there, then the one further on that looked even larger, and the other big one near it ... without realising that I had wandered off the towpath.

I had entered a private driveway whose banks were covered with the largest dandelions I had ever seen. To my dismay two men on tractors had started cutting them. On seeing my half-full basket one of them beckoned me over and told me that I was on the local Water Authority's property, but he smiled and said, 'if I cut the other bank with my mate, could you get enough from this one in say, half an hour?' Could I! I collected enough to make two gallons of wine which I hoped I could rack into jars before the next paying guests arrived; they might not like two plastic buckets standing on the fridge.

We had nearly three weeks before their arrival and Owen thought it a good idea to cruise along the remainder of the canals in the Birmingham Canal Navigation system, the heart of the canal world. An artery of waterways streams out to all points of the compass; famous engineers and architects here vied to build locks, tunnels, bridges, toll houses and offices. Some 160 miles of connecting waterways, along with wharves and basins adjoining the new railways, made this a singularly prosperous part of the water transport system, that worked successfully with the railways up to 1945.

Today, much has been abandoned, leaving stagnant water lanes and desolate buildings. Some canals are navigable – just – and are classified by the BWB as remainder canals, as opposed to cruising canals. If you travel along a remainder canal, be prepared for the worst as obviously only minor maintenance is carried out on them ... and judging by our experience of maintenance on cruising canals, the remainder canals must be classed as a challenge to any boater.

We continued down the Coventry canal, turning off at Fazeley on to the Birmingham and Fazeley. We had explored this junction canal the previous year so apart from picking up our mail at Tyburn, on the Birmingham outskirts, we made only two overnight stops before reaching Spaghetti junction again.

This time we took the Aston route to Birmingham and climbed first the 11 Aston locks which are followed almost immediately by the 13 Farmers Bridge locks. The latter carry you through the centre of the city; indeed as you steer into the dark caverns between concrete pillars of one lock you realise uncomfortably that it is supporting a huge post office tower above.

At the top of the locks lies Cumbrian wharf, the tourist attraction laid out by Birmingham City Corporation and planned in such a way that if you decide to tie up to visit the BWB Information Centre, or the newly-decorated canal pub, you may do so only if not more than three boats are moored outside the pub already. If you tie up on the towpath opposite the pub and BWB Office, the only way to cross the canal is to walk another half a mile, over a bridge and then fight your way back through a maze of backstreets.

It was such a hot day that, after working through all those locks, we gasped for a cool lager and it was only through the kindness of another boater allowing us to breast up alongside him that we could get our ale. As his was a brand new boat, with gleaming sides, I thought it a splendid gesture indeed to let our 65 feet of steel lie beam to beam.

Duly refreshed, we moved on to Gas Street Basin, a few yards round the bend of the canal, where we tied up for the night.

Birmingham failed to tempt us out that evening so we stayed on board reading and listening to the radio, but the desolation around us made it a depressing mooring. After a quick shopping trip to the squalid Bull Ring next morning, we travelled the Worcester and Birmingham canal towards Kings Norton, passing the spot where there had once been a bar erected across the canal as one company's method of extracting tolls from another!.

How quickly Birmingham's face changes on this canal. Enter or leave the city by no other, through the pleasant suburbs of Edgbaston, overlooking the roofs of Birmingham University, passing moored boats which house some of the students.

The model town of Bournville follows, with its neat streets of toytown houses, with toytown railway station on the canal side ... even the railway engines are painted in the factory's house colours. Then, of course, there is the factory itself divided by the canal.

Moored for the night at Kings Norton junction we reconnoitered this surprisingly pleasant little town. Shops are few, (but they include a health food store selling goat's milk yoghourt) and flank the village green, itself fringed with pretty, flowering trees.

Next morning, we turned back to the Gas Street Basin and began in earnest our travels along the BCN. I was to treasure that visit to Kings Norton, the last memorable piece of scenery for two whole weeks.

The passage through Rydal Green locks was sheer misery. Plastic bags and wire fouled the propeller again and again. While waiting in one lock pound for Owen to scrape away the debris from the gate in order to be able to open it, I was conscious of a strong smell of paint. Turning my head, I saw to my horror a fine spray of paint emerging from the worn out filters fitted to a vent at the rear of a factory. There was no escape from the paint spray as it drifted over me and boat. I wonder if factory inspectors ever check externally?

The bridge at the foot of Rydal Green locks is the lowest we had passed under and from the roof of the boat we had to remove all my lettuce plants and flower pots, even the boat pole. I then had to duck unable to see what awaited us the other side. I crouched, steering blindly, but safely.

The next few days presented great contrasts in scenery. After the pollution of Rydal, we crossed by aqueduct at Wednesbury, high in the air beside a new motorway. Then the back gardens of a housing estate before we turned off at the Tame Valley junction. Within minutes, we found the perfect night mooring at Hamstead, a deep unspoilt cutting, with stately trees providing homes for birds and squirrels, complete with an undergrowth sufficiently thick to encourage prowling foxes. Even the water was crystal and we sat outside with a pre-dinner sherry to watch fish and frogs and a friendly water-worm.

Alas beauty was but skin-deep. Within 300 yards of our mooring, next day our still clear water was choked with wooden planks, old barrels, car tyres, and the ubiquitous plastic bloody bag.

We sped – all four knots – through the rest of the Tame Valley canal, slag heaps for our decor. Beneath Spaghetti junction again we realised we had now approached it from all directions. After filming both kinds of transport, motorways and canal, we retraced our afternoon journey, and spent the night in Witton outside the Safe Harbour, which is not a harbour of course, but a pub.

Cottage gardens on one side offered a backdrop to our night's mooring, embankments of industrial waste on the opposite side of the canal provided another.

As I held the rope, waiting for Owen to bring the mooring spikes, a picture of a Grand Old English Gentleman, in the bloom of Good Health, came along the towpath. His rosy face shone as if buffed by a silk scarf, silver hair gleamed immaculatly and he wore a modern purple-striped shirt that complimented his knife-creased grey trousers.

He smiled a greeting, stopped by my side and said 'smell'. I wondered if I'd heard aright, some regional dialects confused me, but he said it again, 'smell'. Did he mean that *I* smelt? He beckoned me over ... I followed. 'Go on, smell – there now isn't it grand?' And it was. The warm perfume of wallflowers. My companion pointed beyond the cottages. 'Go and see them, they're in the cemetery. You'll have to be quick, it shuts at six.'

A yell from Owen asking how far I intended pulling the boat made me realise that I was still attached to the rope – but once we'd tied up, I made a hasty toilet and persuaded him to do the same. 'Quick, I want to go to the cemetery before it closes.' Thankfully, he knows me so well that nothing nowadays surprises him. But Witton Cemetery surprised us both.

A formal entrance of wide stone steps lead up from the canal and road into a cloud of perfume and a riot of colour. Hundreds of wallflowers make a multi-coloured border on either side as they climb too. Flower beds, lawns and gracious old trees faced us at the top. Cemeteries have never done much for me; in fact, I think they are a waste of good earth, but in a park-like atmosphere as at Witton, they have an excuse.

As we returned to the boat, almost drunk with the aroma lingering in the warm April air, I saw my GOEG, by the gate of the end cottage. He had obviously watched us, and now he beamed, 'lovely, that's what they are, lovely.' He pointed to some tombstones showing above the wall opposite his cottage. 'Third from the end – that's my wife's. All we cottagers have been promised a place.'

He invited us in and proudly showed us around. It was a reflection of himself; neat, clean, shining and spotless. He lived alone and did all the housework, laundering and cooking. Brass ornaments on the mantelpiece in the back kitchen gleamed and twinkled in the evening sun. He took up a lovely brass candlestick shaped as a hand, the long graceful fingers holding, almost caressing, the pristine white candle. He smiled when I admired it and said, 'I made the pair of 'em for the wife when we were first wed'. He explained how man and boy he had walked the towpath outside to the engineering foundry where he had worked a couple of miles away. 'I've seen some changes. Years ago, the canal here was higher than the land around – now as you see, it's closed in by embankments of rubbish.' He produced a photo showing a young man with a horse and cart. 'That's my brother; he farmed over there, where that old slag heap is. Matter of fact that's where this was taken.' I looked out of his window at the desolate scene. He had seen some changes indeed.

Next to his cottage was a derelict plot of land, covered with weed and scrubby patches of bramble. 'Oh that,' he followed my gaze. 'That's another modern crackpot idea gone wrong. Now, in the old days, when things went wrong, they did something about it. Take these cottages here. They wouldn't be here if it wasn't for a mistake. Nearly 140 years ago, the cemetery was first laid out proper, and it was decided to surround it with a beautiful brick wall. Best bricks they had to be, good colour as well as texture. Well when they'd finished the wall, they found they'd ordered too many bricks – so they didn't leave 'em lying about. No, they went ahead and built this row of cottages. And now some fool from the Council has decided that the three end ones should be pulled down. Didn't say why or what they were going to put in their place. And they've left that bit to turn into a wilderness for the kids to chuck their rubbish and the parents to throw old beer cans. Worst of all, the weeds blow into my garden.'

Next to see was the garden which like the house was neat and tidy with everything growing just so. I was given a root of mint when I mentioned my roof garden and as he bent down to dig up the mint, Owen commented on the way it seemed to be in what looked like a piece of roof coping, pushed deep into the soil to prevent the roots from wandering. The old man patted the coping gently. 'You'll never guess where that came from – Coventry Cathedral. I was there that night they bombed it and I brought this little bit back as a souvenir, not that I'll ever forget such a night.'

He was certainly a lively and entertaining companion and I just had to invite him on board to spend the evening with us when he kept us regaled with a fund of anecdotes. I'm looking forward to our next visit to Witton; let's hope the wallflowers are in bloom.

30

The Rushall Canal was the next remainder waterway we cruised. The first rain for many weeks accompanied us at the start of the Rushall locks and as this developed into a thunderstorm, we were forced to stay in lock four until it abated. We had five more locks to work through which we hoped to complete by lunchtime.

As we left number eight, we hooted to let people outside the lock ahead of us know we were coming and to leave the gate open for us. They appeared to be startled; like us they must have had a shock meeting other boaters, for they were the first we had encountered since leaving the Birmingham and Worcester canal.

They ran down the towpath towards us so Owen jumped off *Bix* to meet them. He signalled me to slow down and pull in to the side where we were to tie up. When we were firmly moored, he bade me follow him to where three boats sat in an empty lock, empty but for mud, that is. It was the first time I had seen a lock completely drained. People around the boats were tarring, painting and carrying out repairs to the sides and bottoms of their boats. They, we found out, were members of a boating club, situated just outside the top lock. As few used this canal, they had decided to lock in the boats, drain the water and use the resultant dry-dock (well almost dry) to paint underneath their boats. All locks had been closed while repairs were carried out to the gates of the first two, but our arrival coincided with reopening day, and our appearance had upset their plans.

As we were in no hurry, we agreed to wait for a couple of hours which so pleased them that they offered open house at their club bar where we enjoyed the company and entertainment provided. When it was time to enter through the lock, willing helpers ensured a swift and labour-free passage. As we waved goodbye, they yelled a warning, 'after the bend, there's very little water; oh and watch out for the fridge someone's chucked in at the next bridge.'

Because of the lack of water we grounded several times but spotted the fridge in time and glided carefully over its top. The landscape turned industrial with a matching canal. At Brownhills we even welcomed blocks of flats as a break in the monotony. We cleared Catshill and Ogley junctions following the Anglesey branch to Chasewater reservoir where it peters out.

We moored for the night alongside this popular open air leisure centre where, even at seven o'clock, it was still warm enough for toddlers to use the paddling pools. The level of the reservoir, although low, provided enough water for ski boats. The go-kart racing circuit was packed and it was obvious that the inhabitants of surrounding towns also made use of these facilities.

We found it noisy and were glad to return to the peace of the canal.

Early next morning we went back to Catshill junction where we joined the Wyrley and Essington as far as the Cannock extension. For two miles this arm wanders through pleasant rural scenery with views across the wide flat plains to the chimneys of Walsall. At the end of Cannock extension we had difficulty in turning round the boat and had to reverse quite a way back before finding enough space. Although the boat yards lining this part of the canal were open, they seemed unwilling to supply gas or water. We managed however to buy some gas, but the water tap was too congested by boats.

We went back to the Wyrley and Essington and continued to Walsall which we reached by late afternoon, after a most depressing journey through housing estates, wasteland and heavy industry.

We tied up outside an interesting building, with an inscription cut into the stone above the door lintel: Boatman's rest 1900. Even at that late date the canal was still profitable enough to provide an overnight stopping place for boatmen.

We found water outside the top lock at Walsall and the town itself isn't too far away for shopping, although it's uphill all the way back with a heavy basket. It has little charm and only the pigeon houses have been painted in the last ten years. You have to be a pigeon or a fancier to enjoy Walsall.

The afternoon took us through more tracts of depressing industrial wasteland. When we reached the Tame Valley junction, even though we moored outside a power station for the night, we rejoiced in a grassy towpath, and discovered that cooling towers have a special grandeur when viewed through the window by moonlight.

Next day back at Rydals Green, I managed to avoid our paint-spraying friends until at Pudding Green junction we joined the main Birmingham line where we tied up for the night in the arm leading to Netherton Tunnel. It was just that little further from the railway line which runs noisily by the side of the main canal.

We had planned to watch a play on television that night but witnessed a drama much nearer home. Returning from a stroll towards the boat, Owen spotted a red glow alongside it. Running back he discovered that a rubbish tip in the back of a factory was on fire, which spread quickly to the surrounding grass and hedges.

He yelled to me to fetch a bucket and help damp down the blaze. Owen ran to the factory, to call for help while I tried to prevent the flames leaping through the railings to fire the towpath. I suddenly realised that adjoining the burning rubbish was a mountain of polythene mouldings, close to our boat. Flames crept through the fence to light the brittle grasses on the towpath edge.

Should I move the boat? Where had Owen gone? The flames leapt high into bushes and young trees and the bridge across the entrance of the arm were alight so I could not take the boat out backwards. How would a fire engine reach the blaze if the bridge caught alight?

Owen finallly returned to help beat out the burning towpath. He had climbed a fence to reach the night watchman, about a quarter of a mile along the towpath. The nightwatchman did not want to know. 'We often burn rubbish down there,' he said. Even when told of the magnitude of the fire, he still refused help so Owen ran on to the main road and stopped a car, which drove him to the nearest phone box where he could summon the fire brigade.

Sirens and blue flashing lights soon appeared on the opposite side of the canal but by the time they reached the bridge it was burning fiercely. Soon a hose was run out and water streamed on to the blazing bushes and bridge from which burning planks were torn and thrown into the canal to expire with a hiss and a shower of golden sparks.

It was 10.30 before the firemen rolled up their hoses and returned to station. We had fought the fire for two and a half hours and although the boat as well as ourselves were dirty and smoke-begrimed, at least we still had a home.

As we prepared to move off next morning, we saw a group of bowler hatted men, standing by the remains of the fire. One asked in a haughty tone, 'You there, do you know anything about this fire?' While Owen went over to speak to them, I stayed on board as I felt my temper rising. I only hope he told them what he thought of their night security system, especially the notices warning about guard dogs patrolling the premises, as not one had appeared even when the firemen were busy with hoses and ladders on several parts of the company's property.

Our journey now followed the Birmingham main line where for the first time since starting on the remainder canals, we saw another boat. On the whole, our journey was dull, railway giving place to industry. The 'floating islands' that appeared now and again were the remains of toll offices which demanded payment according to weight and cargo. The buildings are gone, leaving only the oval-shaped foundations which scare some boaters, who wonder whether to bear to the right or left. We usually took the right hand channel but sometimes found ourselves firmly stuck on a shelf just below water. It takes quite a bit of pushing, grunting and heaving to get *Bix* clear of such obstacles. Why doesn't the BWB erect notices indicating the best channel?

We completed the not very prepossessing Wryley and Essington canal, by mooring outside the Boatman's Rest in Walsall. I would have liked to have seen inside this little building but, an office now, it was closed each time we arrived. I would have preferred a different mooring for the night but, too late, we had to sleep near a noisy club, 20 yards away, which quietened only after midnight.

After a hasty turnround next morning we retraced our path towards Wolverhampton where a second visit to the theatre put me in a better frame of mind. It was the lure of the rural canals that made us navigate the 21 Wolverhampton locks as fast as we could. They took three hours and oh the bliss on leaving the last one to emerge on to the lovely Stafford and Worcester canal.

At Compton, two miles on, we relaxed that evening listening to birdsong and admiring the greenery of trees and grass and bush. Mind you, with the cuckoo still cucking at 10 o'clock that night I grew fidgety and even more irritated when the moorhens decided to squabble at two in the morning. Half an hour later, we woke to a tapping noise, along the length of the boat. It was a staccato tap, tap, tap. I began to feel frightened. ... Owen rose and looked out of the window to the alarm of half a dozen mallards which promptly took flight.

'Last night a load of drunks, tonight, bloody ducks,' Owen muttered. Still he had to admit it was easier to get rid of the ducks.

31

We picked up our second paying guests from Autherley junction for this part of the canal system is both attractive and offers a variety of routes to other canals. The main reason for choosing Autherley this time, however, was that, unusually, it was one of the few places where a car could drive alongside the boat. And this was vital because Joe, one of our new guests, was severely handicapped.

The first letter told us that Clara was 79 and Joe 70, that they would so much like a boating holiday but that Joe was handicapped, having no use of the left side of his body and able to walk only if supported, and then only at a slow shuffle. Their main worry was the bed: if it was a bunk bed then Joe could not get in or out.

As ours was an ordinary double bed this presented no problem but, and it was a big but, how would Joe get about the boat? We wrote back and forth and were soon convinced that they could manage satisfactorily once Joe was aboard.

A friend drove them from Liverpool to Autherley, and with Owen's help Joe was carried on board. Clara, belying her 79 years, stepped sprightly on to *Bix* unaided. Joe knew that he was on *Bix* until the end of the week, as I was not strong enough to help Owen get him ashore. But that didn't worry him and after a few hours in his lively company it didn't worry us.

Joe was keen to cruise through the Potteries and so we repeated our journey along the canal towards Great Haywood Junction (pages 113, 114) and there joined the Trent and Mersey. I steered while Owen worked the locks, as we did when travelling alone, because Joe and Clara could take no part in handling the boat at all. They were content to sit out front where they took a great interest in what was happening. They themselves caused interest as boating is not a popular holiday for people in their seventies.

Grey, drizzly weather forced them below where Joe who had already discovered the bookshelves, was soon into *Evelyn's Diary*, a book he had wanted to read for many years. Clara concentrated on her knitting, which was beautiful and neat.

Our evenings were spent playing chess or their recently discovered Scrabble. Gradually, we learnt their life stories, how Joe had been handicapped from babyhood and went to school in the east end of London until he was fourteen. He found that he had a gift for languages and learned French at night school. Soon he was proficient in German, Belgian and Dutch. So good did he become that he found himself running a language class where he met Clara. A wartime censor and now retired he worked from home as a part-time interpreter. For stimulation, only three months earlier, he had decided to learn Chinese! A modern day George Borrow if ever I met one.

I found the days tiring, what with extra cooking, entertaining and working the boat, but the week with Joe and Clara was a happy one.

From Great Haywood, the Trent and Mersey flows through pleasant meadows, after which parkland and villages soon appear. Weston, Salt and Sandon slip by almost unnoticed as they lie slightly off the canal. At Stone, however, you are in a real canal town, with boatyards, dry docks and locks as scenery until the railway draws so close that it becomes impossible to find a quiet mooring for the night.

As you approach Stoke, power stations and railways dominate until another rural stretch takes over, leading quietly past the Wedgwood factory at Barlaston which is open to the public for tours and the opportunity to buy their famous wares. We continued our journey through desolation to Stoke on Trent. Here all the bridges were so low that we had to slow down and remove both flower pots and TV aerial. Stoke offered no relaxation as extensive roadworks were in progress adjoining the canal. Occasionally, the towpath disappeared to become a trench, a hole for a concrete pillar, or just plant dump for a new motorway was under construction, together with a new canal. Already a new lock, with modern lockhouse was complete, nigh to Stoke railway station, and according to the workmen, ours was the first boat to pass through.

Although it was May and holidays had started, this part of the canal was less popular than the section that kept to the countryside for Harecastle tunnel, two miles further on, was closed for repairs. This meant that boats had to turn and retrace their passage through Stoke, a fate worse than any death.

But Joe and Clara were amused by the sight of Doulton ware: lavatories, basins, pedestals, not only white but in pastel shades as well. Their serried rows had not been envisaged by Joe when he had expressed a desire to sail through the potteries.

There is an alternative for boaters who want to avoid the tunnel-and-back trip: about a mile past Stoke, the Caldon Canal has been restored recently and provides a further twenty miles of Wedgwood country to explore before turning back at Leek or Consall Forge.

The Caldon starts at the town of Etruria, named after the house where Josiah Wedgwood first lived but sadly there is little left of the original town. Although a few bottle kilns remain forlorn and lonely, the original Etruria factory is a ruin flanking the canal. Petitions to the local council failed to save Etruria, although it may have helped preserve an old flint and bone mill a few yards on. As we chugged by, we greeted the workmen re-roofing the building, and whose chimney proudly carries both its name and purpose. Soon, the mill will house a museum of pottery and provide some recompense for the loss of a living museum.

Before leaving the Trent and Mersey for the Caldon, we had navigated another new lock where workmen were still finishing off the towpath. They tipped us off about water. We were not in the habit of checking the route of a new canal before travelling along it. During the winter months, we made a note of locks under repair etc. but in summer, boating was usually straightforward with little or no problems.

However, we gladly took our friendly workmen's advice and topped up with water and emptied our Elsan at the sanitary station by the junction of the Caldon and the Trent and Mersey at Etruria. Neither service is available on the Caldon Canal.

The Caldon's start forewarns of what's to follow: even if you have no idea in which direction you are facing! It twists, turns and loops the loop. As there was little water our 65 footer took some navigating round the bends. Two locks greet you at the start followed by a fairly well landscaped cement works, followed by another lock. Leaving this, we decided it was the ideal place for Joe and Clara to be picked up at the end of their holiday: a BWB yard with an entrance to the main Hanley road abutted the canal.

We stopped the boat to establish our location vis-a-vis the road and soon I noticed an elderly man looking at my lettuce plants on the boat's roof. He was a mine of information about gardening and, more important, about local shops. He mentioned a launderette 100 yards from the bridge, an added bonus.

With their last two days with us Joe and Clara decided to explore the Caldon for a day and then return to Planet lock ready for pick up.

The canal divides the lovely grounds of Hanley Park into two, with shrubs and bushes on both sides and a particularly decorative iron bridge across the canal. Access to the park from the canal is impossible but the gates are not too far from either Planet lock bridge or bridge number six.

We moored in the park reach for afternoon tea, whereupon a crowd gathered on the bridge to watch us eat: obviously not many boats come along this canal. As we were about to start our tea, I noticed my new friend from the lock so we set another place and invited him to join us. I fetched another cup and saucer and returned to find him conversing with Joe in French, German and even Flemish. Joe loved every moment of it as did our new friend. Owen, who is fluent in French, made it a trio.

What a surprise tea party that turned out to be. Our new friend had been born in Hanley and during the first world war had married a Belgian and lived in that country for many years. Now a widower, he had returned to Hanley to live with his daughter. He loved the canal where he walked daily to feed the ducks and keep the towpath tidy.

His visit coincided with the end of Joe and Clara's holiday. That night we moored at Foxley, some three miles from Hanley, and had our final game of Scrabble. Clara also presented me with a knitting pattern for socks without heels!

After seeing them off at Planet Lock I had time for the launderette and to give the boat a quick clean up ready for our next visitor arriving that afternoon: our eldest daughter Rebecca who was to spend a week's convalescence with us after a short stay in hospital.

128

32

With Rebecca happily on board, we set off to explore the Caldon canal from top to tail. Alas we were facing the wrong way.

Two incidents invariably surprise newcomers to *Bix* and our daughter proved no exception. As most visitors come by car we arrange to park the vehicles with a friendly publican nearby. At the visit's end, Owen pulls out our folding bikes and offers to cycle back with our visitor for the car. Horror! 'What, cycle all that way?' When it finally sinks in that they have travelled only five or six miles during the whole trip and that the route by road may be shorter than a twisting canal – they feel a little foolish and kick themselves for failing to appreciate what is now obvious.

The second surprise is when we haul out a map if we decide to reverse course. A canoe can turn in a canal but *Bix* needs a 'winding hole', where the canal side has been cut away and dredged to allow a 70-foot boat to turn. We keep our fingers crossed that it is still in use and not choked with weeds and rubbish.

As we faced the wrong way it was necessary to go back through the first three locks to enable us to turn at the junction. What with taking in water, emptying the Elsan, shallow water and strong winds, by the time we had turned *Bix* and navigated the locks yet again, the day was almost over. Rebecca was amazed to spend her first night aboard half a mile up canal from where she had joined us four hours earlier.

Had the weather behaved itself, the Caldon would have been perfect for convalescing. After two days of bitter winds we longed for sunshine. On Wednesday it brightened by which time we had reached Hazelhurst junction where the canal divides to Leek, or Consall Forge. Scenery is varied from industries at the beginning, mostly potteries. Here for the first time in our travels, we saw the canal used for the purpose for which is was designed – to carry pottery. Two boats daily ferry plates, cups, saucers, jugs, from pottery to packing department, three miles away. The china is carried in wire baskets without protection: straight from work bench to basket, to boat, then a steady 2 mph and unload from boat to packer. Breakages negligible and time mimimal compared with wrapping each item and transporting by lorry.

Rebecca is a potter and wanted to visit a factory: alas none allowed this.

It was fascinating travelling at our leisurely pace with time to peep through windows and see perhaps 200 toby jugs awaiting paint, or a row of cats with newly-daubed coats.

Soon the factories and the ridiculously low bridges give way to open country and locks that raise you 500 feet above sea level.

We chose the Leek branch at the junction where we glided between beautiful old trees to enter a serpentine section of water. The canal widens into a lake outside Leek tunnel, where we had to turn, as only small boats can navigate the waters beyond it.

The woods were full of birds and the canal had its share of swans, moorhens and mallard warming in the sun. Rebecca and I took a bus from Horse bridge number six to shop in Leek. One of the canal's great engineers, James Brindley, had a millwright's business here and in the market, I found a book with the name Brindley on the fly-leaf, sadly not James. Although it was market day most stalls sold clothes; we found none offering local farm products.

When following the contours, as the Caldon canal does, it is possible to travel a few miles and moor opposite your starting point separated by a field. More strange even is to see a boat high above you through the trees, (if you are on the Consall branch), or conversely if on the Leek branch, you gaze way, way down at the vessels below.

We returned from Leek through Hazlehurst junction to Cheddleton where a well-preserved flint mill attracts tourists, by boat and car. At the mill-side stand two picture postcard cottages on whose stone walls the sun shone brightly: the more bewildering therefore as we walked beneath the bridge to find bats overhead, the first time I had seen bats in daytime. There were plenty here oblivious of or indifferent to the sun outside.

Towards Consall Forge, the River Churnet runs parallel with the canal. Thick woods spread down to the edge of the canal and the birdsong echoed over the water to the river. It was a particularly beautiful part of the canal, even the names – Woods lock and Oak Meadow Ford lock – were in keeping with the scenery. Once through Oak Meadow the canal widens: the River Churnet has been canalised.

Where this happens elsewhere you can tell by the water which flows, as distinct from a canal where current is negligible. Secondly, the water is clearer. This is noticeable where the Oxford canal joins the River Cherwell: I swear you can see a demarcation line in the water.

And you can in beautiful Consall Woods, but alas reversed, by which I mean that the river not the canal has the dirty water. Sailing on thick black ink, surrounded by sunlit flowers and trees is an Alice's wonderland indeed.

At the limit of navigation for us – Consall Forge – we turned before tying up for afternoon tea. We encountered a small boat that had just returned from Flint Mill Lock, about three-quarters of a mile further along, which was as far as they could manage.

So back through the woods on Charon's water to moor for the night at Basford Bridge where, next morning, the black water was all explained. The 'ink' is waste from a mill further up the Churnet. 'It's much better now, they had so many complaints they were forced to do something about it.' I was told. I wonder what it was like before the complaints?

We returned to Hanley and Planet lock where I decided to do some shopping. Rebecca was due home the next day and we wanted to moor close to Stoke station so that she should catch her train. As Rebecca and I left the store near the bridge who should be waiting for us but my nice old man from Hanley Park. His news was sad: the ducklings he fed each day were now orphans as a young boy had shot the adult duck with an air rifle. I know the BWB have by-laws prohibiting guns and rifles but why waste money on notices when there is no supervision to enforce those by-laws.

We found time to take Rebecca along the Trent and Mersey canal to the Harecastle tunnel entrance, not a pretty canal this, but interesting for its associations with the potteries and the early canal days. A few bottle kilns remain, but the most dramatic point is where the canal passes through a steel works, which must be impressive by night with the furnaces afire. We had the place almost to ourselves as it was Saturday afternoon, gliding past a ghost town of metal sheets, and empty boats, with the odd light bulb glowing dully through dusty yellow office windows.

The remains of the old Wedgwood Pottery at Burslem are few indeed, and Tunstall, the mother town of the six towns that make up the potteries, lies too far off the canal to make exploration easy.

At Harecastle tunnel, we had to turn because of repairs. The three tunnels through Harecastle Hill parallel to each other have always posed problems.

The first, one and three quarter miles long, was built by James Brindley over the course of eleven years and completed in 1777. This was quite a feat in those days: provision of a towpath for the horses to pull the boats was beyond their capabilities so boats had to be 'legged' through, 'leggers' being men who hired themselves out to boat owners and who by lying on planks of wood projecting from the boat 'walked' it through using the roof and tunnel sides. An arduous and dangerous task.

As traffic increased 'legging' caused considerable delay to cargo. So in 1822 Thomas Telford was asked to build a second tunnel alongside Mr Brindley's, this time with a towpath. This was finished in 1827. The first tunnel was used by boats going in one direction, the second by those proceeding in the opposite direction.

But mining subsidence at the start of the century caused the closure of the Brindley tunnel. Mr Telford's tunnel is still in use, but requires much maintenance.

The third, a railway tunnel, was built much later but this too has been abandoned. Today's trains circumnavigate Harecastle Hill.

The tunnel water is a mixture of grey-orange and green which, say locals, is due to ironstone in the soil. All I know is that when we dipped in the boat pole, the water drops were iridescent green and as they plopped back into the canal, an orangey slime rose to the surface.

Next morning we said a sad farewell to Rebecca, hoping that it wouldn't be too long before we saw her and the rest of the family again.

We meandered down the Trent and Mersey, alone again en route to the North and North West canals, which meant Autherley junction once more.

The days passed slowly and we caught up with our correspondence, articles and lecture notes; sometimes we just sat in the sun irritated that it hadn't been like this for Rebecca.

Late Friday morning, we reached Gailey Wharf and while I prepared lunch, Owen asked for casual work at a nearby boatyard. We were the answer to his prayers, said the owner who had four boats returning that afternoon to be cleaned and prepared for the next hirers that evening ... and both his regular cleaners were unavailable.

By four o'clock that afternoon, Owen and I had earned £5.40: the boats were ready and we had made another business contact.

33

The Shropshire Union canal started life as the Shropshire Union Railway and Canal Company, the original plan being to build a railway on the existing canal bed. Luckily the plan was abandoned and the canal was dug instead. At first it was the property of the London and North Western Railway, then that of the London Midland and Scottish Railway, all of which it survived to become the holidaymaker's favourite canal, The Shroppie.

Earlier we had hired holiday boats here and excitably recalled each well-loved beauty spot. The first few miles from Autherley junction skirt Wolverhampton Aerodrome; the Wolverhampton Boat Club occupies a goodly stretch of water; then the lush green countryside reappears near Brewood, itself the highlight of many a canal cruise. The character of this attractive village stems from its clusters of Georgian houses, friendly pubs and of course the canal running through a heavily-wooded cutting. It was here that I saw my first kingfisher on that long remembered boating holiday.

From Brewood to Norbury junction, the canal scenery alternates. One moment you are in woods, then for a mile an embankment reveals wide vistas of flat countryside. A small tunnel at Cowley leads to the village of Gnosall, a place I've never dared attempt to pronounce!

Norbury junction doesn't! The Newport branch connecting with the Shropshire Union here is now unnavigable so traffic heads for Market Drayton, some fifteen miles away.

The canal drifts through open farm land, passing the tiny hamlet of High Offley with its two pubs, one opening only three days a week while the other, standing virtually in the churchyard, has somewhat more normal opening times.

After ten miles free of locks, the five Tyrley locks remind you that this is a canal and work beckons.

The Tyrleys are beautifully looked after and a joy to use. It makes locking so less strenuous when balance beams respond to a touch, paddles work smoothly and when the verges and towpath are free of nettles and pot-holes.

Market Drayton was a stopover for shopping and job-hunting. Here was a town with a street market taking precedence over the motor car! Marvellous. Stalls and shoppers thronged the long narrow street defying even a bicycle to approach. How many years had it been since I last saw fresh farm food sold by the grower direct to the public? One man offered fresh spinach, a few cabbage plants and watercress, shiny with glistening

133

waterdrops still on the leaves. At most he had £5 of produce to sell, but still found it worthwhile to come to town on market day. I bought the last of the spinach and some watercress. Before midday had struck, he was sold out and off.

On our way back to the boat we passed the Labour Exchange so Owen went in to see about vacancies. After reading the various cards advertising jobs, he applied to the clerk for one. 'You wouldn't like that – it's very hard work,' she said, 'and dirty.' Owen said he would still like an interview, but again she put forward an objection. 'You have to be there very early in the morning.' By now, Owen was angry. He leaned across the desk and for a moment I thought he was about to hit her! Instead he pointed to some paper and asked for the phone number and name of the person to contact. Five minutes later, he left the phone box outside, smiling. 'I've got the job, start seven o'clock on Monday. It's a stone crushing mill.'

The job was near Kidsgrove and so we had to travel further than normal each day to be on target that Sunday night.

We left Market Drayton after lunch and passed through the five Addersley locks by late afternoon, mooring for the night just short of the Audlem locks as we knew we could not get through all 15 of them before the 5.30 pm closing time. Next morning we were first to make the 90 foot descent to farmland level. Cows kept us company for four or five miles to Nantwich, with its attractive timbered houses.

Nantwich was the main salt centre from Roman times to the 19th century. It also prospered from the canal. Nantwich basin was the terminus of the Chester canal into which Telford planned to run the Birmingham and Liverpool junction canal. The owner of Dorfold Park refused to surrender land so the canal had to be built high on an embankment round the park. Today the old cheese warehouses in the basin have been restored, and a boat hire company and boat club thrive there.

At Barbridge junction, we forsook the Shroppie in favour of the Middlewich branch as we wanted to cruise the Trent and Mersey canal. The ten-mile link between the two canals is quietly rural. Church Minshull is its only local village and this is nearer the River Weaver than the canal.

Middlewich is another salt town and a small one. I had expected a large bustling town, but instead I passed through the shopping centre without realising it! Mining subsidence has prevented major development, although new engineering methods offer some hope for the future.

Once on the Trent and Mersey, we headed for Kidsgrove, at the far end of Harecastle tunnel, past salt works, salt mines and brine pools. Subsidence causes towpaths to sink. The different layers of concrete where the towpath has been built up are noticeable from the boat. Between Anderton and Middlewich, a new canal was dug as subsidence had breached the old.

There are eight locks at Wheelock, another six between there and Rode Heath, and a further eleven from there to Kidsgrove. Heartbreak Hill, the waterman calls this stretch and as we struggled through the last of them, I was in heartfelt sympathy with him.

The locks are in pairs, but in almost every case only one lock works and no method has been found to tell boaters which lock to use. It's no fun heading for the wrong gates only to reverse and straighten in time to approach the other lock.

Subsidence has affected this part of the canal. At Rode Heath, the BWB built an all-steel lock, designed to resist subsidence. Its gaunt steel skeleton stands useless today while thousands of boaters continue to use the stubborn gates and nigh immovable paddles of its hundred-year-old partner.

But we managed it all and moored near the BWB yard at Red Bull on the outskirts of Kidsgrove. All we had to do now was to locate the small village of Harmers End five miles away, where Owen was due to start work next day in the local stone-crushing mill.

Each year, in company with other factories in the area, they closed for potters' fortnight as it was called. This was the time for maintenance and cleaning to be carried out by casual labour. Next morning Owen left at six to give himself plenty of time to find the mill. As our mail was due to be collected I cycled to Kidsgrove post office, a mile and a half away. Conditions were tropical as I sweated up the hill into town. Back aboard *Bix* the thermometer read an unbelievable 102F. I spent the rest of the day outside in a cool spot near the lock where I typed away the afternoon.

When Owen returned at 7.30 that evening I hardly recognised him. Covered from head to toe in grey dust ... he outlined the day's work from the shower. His gang of labourers were detailed to clean the stone crushing machinery and the insides of the chimneys.

I wondered how he would last the next few days. He was accustomed to heavy farm work but surely not as heavy as this job sounded. But the gang were splendid to work with and he was sure he would enjoy it.

Two weeks' casual work turned into four, with more if we had wanted it, twelve hours a day Monday to Friday with five or six hours more on Saturdays and Sundays. Even the £90 weekly wage packet failed to ease my mind as I thought of Owen 90 feet up a chimney, scraping away the brickdust.

I sought work in Kidsgrove too, but there was no typing agency, few shops and fewer offices. I soon discovered that miners' fortnight followed the potters' fortnight and the factories were shut too. Even the local buses abandoned the published timetable during these holiday periods making it difficult to plan trips to nearby towns.

Although alone every day until the evening, I found plenty to do. I had my writing, and as there was an abundance of wild life, I spent every afternoon with my binoculars at different places along the towpath. Before long I settled into a routine and became part of the neighbourhood. Walking the towpath each day revealed the regulars with one or two of whom I became friendly, and so life became static again for a few weeks.

34

Of the towpath regulars a young married couple walked the baby and dog each evening from the bridge to the third lock, where the dog would jump into the water after sticks. When he scrambled out he covered the man with water, to baby's delight.

And then there was 'Erbert who stopped each morning at *Bix* for a chat. The lettuces on the roof of the boat caught his eye. The fierce heat of the sun above and the burning steel below had virtually destroyed them. As I tipped them into the hedgerow, 'Erbert told me to go 'to third 'ouse oop bank' where I could buy lettuces from the garden. I found it difficult to understand his dialect even when he didn't use local words like 'bank' meaning 'hill,' for all hills around here, large or small, are banks. And there seems to be a bank around every corner. I've never seen so many switchback main roads, side streets and lanes. I reckon the towpath is the flattest part of Kidsgrove.

I missed 'Erbert for a few days, but met him shopping one Saturday. 'It's been that 'ot,' he explained and I didn't blame him when I saw the bank he had to climb to his home. He promised me a treat on Monday morning and all the weekend I wondered what it would be.

Owen had got fed up with my constant talk of 'Erbert so in defence brought two workmates back to the boat that Saturday afternoon. We planned to recharge the water tanks, empty the Elsan and check the diesel, all regular weekly chores. This involved 200 yards, plus a further half a mile and two locks before we could turn the boat and head back to our mooring! For our visitors a joy trip, but I often wonder how many of them would accept our primitive life on a permanent basis. Almost everyone says he envies us, but ...

Our Saturday afternoon visitors tried steering *Bix* and, of course, worked the locks. Canal traffic built up as the holidaymakers hiring from the two adjacent boatyards set off on their week's cruising. Most of them worry when they see our 65 feet but as they pass, they relax gradually and we see them tug their new captain's cap at a jaunty angle!

Monday came – with 'Erbert who wanted to show me something that all of England should be proud of. Intrigued, I accompanied him some distance up a bank, past a terrace of grey houses, one or two of which had been turned into shops. There he stopped and pointed.

We faced an identical terrace, one house of which carried an inscription carved in a stone slab above the door, which read, 'R J Mitchell – designer of the Spitfire. Born here 20.5.1895.' 'Erbert almost burst with pride. 'There, you didn't expect that did you?' I didn't and for once I felt lost for words. I managed to say that Ian, my son-in-law, and an aeroplane enthusiast, would be green with envy. I too now swelled with pride as I realised how honoured I was to have 'Erbert as a friend and guide.

When I told Owen about it later that evening, he said he supposed 'Erbert would go to the top of my collection. Collection? 'Yes, you've been collecting old men ever since we've been on the canals.'

I sat and counted − well, yes there had been the old chap on the Pontcysyllte aqueduct, when we had hired a boat for a holiday on the Llangollen Canal. Then there was the retired BWB man at Long Buckby, and another old waterman I'd met at Braunston. There was the not-so-old ex-Navy man who now built boats on the Gloucester and Sharpness. He had let us use his water tap last winter; and then there were all those nice bridgemen I'd talked to on my walks on the same canal. And, of course, Mr Hanley Park who had shown me the launderette and shops. And now I had 'Erbert. I thought it a collection to be proud of. They had all helped me in so many ways and I had lots of memories about all of them. But outstanding amongst them all, is what happened because of that first meeting with the old man at Llangollen.

The Llangollen Canal attracts so many visitors that it gets more like the M1 each day, or so I'm told by other boaters. We've not been on it for years, but if it's true, then none has gone there because of my recommendation. Only once did I suggest a holiday on the Llangollen. I had returned from this Welsh canal full of the peace, and tranquillity, the beauty of the countryside and extolling the famous Pontcysyllte aqueduct, surely the most spectacular attraction of the whole canal system.

I was talking about my holiday to my dentist who became so interested that he decided to take his family for a holiday on the canal. I told him about the old man I'd met on the aqueduct and described this incredible piece of engineering, standing 120 feet high above the River Dee and 1,000 feet long. Really it is no more than an iron trough containing enough water to allow a narrow boat to cruise gently across.

A towpath two feet wide constitutes one side, but the other edge is simply the lip of the rim, a mere three inches wide. My old man told me that not only his great grandfather, but his great grandmother had helped build the aqueduct. The women had soaked Welsh wool in sugar which was used as a sandwich between the girders. True or not, I thought it a lovely story. I hoped my dentist would meet him and perhaps find out a little more.

On my next visit my dentist, a pointed instrument in hand said, 'I've you to thank for a really breath-taking holiday,' and launched forthwith into a description of the sort of holiday he, his wife and three-year-old son had had. They had chartered a boat and had navigated the Llangollen and, yes they had crossed the aqueduct. His wife was steering while he was below getting his camera when she screamed that their son had tumbled overboard.

My dentist rushed on deck and saw the boy sitting quite unharmed in the two or three feet of water, which was all that the trough held. The boat chugged forward steadily as father jumped overboard and paddled back to his son, picked him up, shambled out of he water and ran back to the boat. While his wife changed the child's clothes father took over the steering. Suddenly, he called desperately for his wife. 'For God's sake, come up here, QUICK.' She did, to find her husband, ashen-faced and shaking. Without a word, he walked down to the cabin and poured himself a very stiff neat scotch. Then he returned to his wife and said, 'I've just realised that I was not on the towpath when I ran back to the boat with the lad?'

He had run along the narrow iron rim of the aqueduct, 120 feet above the rushing, gurgling River Dee.

So now you know why I never tell anyone about the Llangollen canal.

Our stay at Kidsgrove was drawing to an end and it finished spectacularly. Four or five months earlier I had written about *Bix* and us for a famous woman's magazine who had accepted it. Now passing boats called out our name; some even stopped to photograph us. Before long the editor was sending us fan mail and I began to wonder what I had started, especially one letter. It read 'to say that your article has completely changed our life is putting it mildly.' I certainly hadn't meant to change other people's lives. As I write this, a year later, I still meet people who want to discuss that article.

For me our last day was sad. I had been watching a moorhen with her four chicks swimming lazily alongside the boat. Suddenly, mum squawked furiously, splashed her wings and darted from the bank to the middle of the canal, then back to the bank again. She continued to call out and swim hurriedly back and forth for about three minutes – with no signs of her chicks. She quietened slowly and made for the bank where first one chick, then another emerged from beneath the overhanging bramble. Immediately she swam off with these two chicks: the other pair had fallen victim to the large black cat I'd seen lying asleep in the undergrowth. Do birds have feelings? Was she as sad as I felt? That's something my bird book doesn't tell me.

Owen finished his job on Saturday when we were joined by our son Jan for a week's holiday. I'm sure Owen felt like relaxing too. That's how we treated the next week anyway. We didn't spend lavishly, for although Owen's wage was £90 per week, he received nothing like this because he was on an emergency tax code. Oh, I know he'll get it back – but when?

35

What never ceases to interest me about canals is their pattern of contrast. At Kidsgrove, the Trent and Mersey water is a murky yellow, especially near the winding hole which is so choked with weeds and rubbish that it is now impossible to turn a boat there.

We left Kidsgrove at 2.30 on Saturday and in a quarter of an hour were on the Macclesfield canal, deep into the countryside with water that, if shallow, was at least clear enough to see the weeds, plants and, of course, debris gliding beneath.

Most of the Macclesfield canal is a conservation area, and we so enjoyed its 27 miles, that we travelled up and down it several times during the next three months! This first week with Jan was pleasant, as we basked in the sun.

There are many scenic highspots en route, Mow Cop is the first after Kidsgrove, National Trust property some 1,100 feet atop a hill. It looks like a ruin, standing gaunt and bare with the sky showing through the gaps in the walls and tower. It *is* a ruin; it was built to imitate a ruin in 1750. By the early 19th century it was discovered by the methodists who used it as a preaching centre.

For the next four or five miles until the canal widens out into Congleton Wharf, the countryside is tranquil and beautiful. The waters then narrow to bear you across a small aqueduct, over the road into Congleton.

Snake or roving bridges are a feature of most canals, but those on the Macclesfield are particularly beautiful. These bridges occur where the towpath changes sides, enabling the tug horse to cross without being untied.

Bosley locks are the only flight on this canal. There are twelve of them, all a joy to use thanks to the lock-keeper's maintenance. His hedgetrimming is a work of art, too.

A wooded section, reminiscent of the Oxford canal, follows shortly and lo you are high up above the Macclesfield rooftops. But now it was time to retrace our path and take Jan back to Kidsgrove. Having whetted his appetite, he arranged to take over *Bix* for another week later in the year whilst we were lecturing.

Within a week, we were passing through Macclesfield on our way to Bollington, once again finding ourselves high above the houses of this village built on the sides of several hills. The last ten miles of the Macclesfield takes you through open countryside, an old mill here and there still standing majestically alongside the canal. Some are in use, although not as originally planned.

The Macclesfield ends at Marple junction and the Peak Forest canal joins. Recently reopened, this canal now enables boaters to navigate the Cheshire Ring, a round trip embracing the Trent and Mersey, Bridgewater, Ashton, Rochdale and Macclesfield canals.

We decided to take the shortest length of the Peak Forest canal, about seven and a half miles from Marple to Whaley Bridge. From the moment we turned right at Marple and slowly saw the dramatic scenery of the moors develop, with their stone walls ribboning into the distance I knew that this was our kind of place. Our explorations over the ensuing eight weeks, proved how right I was.

We were to cruise, walk and motor this part of the country many, many times. Marple to Whaley Bridge, then on to Chapel-en-le Frith and Castleton, Buxton and Ashbourne.

As for Whaley Bridge itself – well! ! Whaley Bridge – I love you! From the moment I walked along your only main road and saw the clock outside the magnificent stone Engineering Institute, I fell for you. The clock reveals two faces, one up and one down the High Street and never the twain shall tell the same time. Better still, never shall either tell you the correct time! For time doesn't matter in Whaley Bridge, bypassed by the world despite the juggernauts thundering past the small shops strung out along the road. If the proposed by-pass is ever built, then surely Whaley Bridge must be renamed Paradise.

It is so refreshingly different from any other town we know, so full of character and how much to do there. Each day, yet another poster, written in coloured felt pen, advertises a knitting club, an amenities society, a canal talk, the co-op choir, youth club, nursery school, brass band concert. Why Whaley Bridge is even so old fasioned as to offer the ultimate luxury – a chair by the side of the counter, where you can sit and relax while waiting to be served. Do you recall when each shop had its chair by the counter?

We both found part-time work in Whaley – at the new boatyard in the canal terminus. I helped turn around the hire boats at the weekends while Owen had a most rewarding and fascinating, if somewhat strenuous, job. The building had once been the hub of a busy workboat loading wharf. Trains from the Pennines brought lime into this building, as did the canal. Here the boats awaited their cargoes of lime for onward shipment across the canal network.

Owen dug and pick-axed his way through years of stone and cement to uncover the original rails running along the shed floor. For this building was about to become the waterways living museum. As the weeks went by so more rails appeared; so did the photographers and canal enthusiasts. The waterways grapevine worked fast auguring well for the future of this museum and art gallery.

Reluctantly we agreed to move on from Whaley Bridge as we still had the rest of the Peak Forest canal to explore. In our hearts we knew we would return.

The 16 Marple locks follow the junction and although restored only in the last two years, they still need a fair amount of maintenance. However, they descend 210 feet dramatically with breath-taking views of the distant moors and the River Goyt valley; it's a journey well worth making.

At the foot stands the Marple–Manchester railway viaduct, close alongside the Marple Aqueduct which crosses high above the River Goyt. The view from a train must be superb as you look across to the boats, almost on a level with the train, the river running through thick woodland far below.

Once past this spot, alas, the Peak Forest canal deteriorates for the next seven or eight miles, through Romiley and Hyde until it collapses at Dunkinfield junction where the Ashton canal takes over.

Mills and factories dominate this stretch through the Ashton locks, with one, just one, factory which has landscaped its canal front. For this small oasis in the desert of muck, we rendered thanks. The Ashton locks make hard work for a crew of one, as they require an extra key. The padddles are locked to an iron bar, which must be unfastened and then refastened after use, a preventitive measure against vandals, we were told. Although warned to be on the look out for trouble as we neared Manchester, our trip was peaceful.

We had intended to leave the Ashton canal and join the Rochdale canal for which a special licence is required. The canal had closed half an hour before our arrival, to our annoyance – justifiable, we thought.

Although we appreciate repairs to locks and bridges are necessary, the Rochdale Canal Company knew we were coming and even when to expect us, as the Ashton lock-keeper told us that the word had come down that we were on our way.

There was only one thing to do now and that was turn and retrace our passage to Kidsgrove and Middlewich. There we could pick up the other half of the Trent and Mersey which would take us to the Bridgewater Canal, meeting up with the Rochdale at the other end.

Before setting out on this marathon trip, we wanted to explore that foreign territory known as Manchester. So we turned the boat and moored a little further up the Ashton canal at a spot quieter than the large car park alongside the canal at the Rochdale locks, and where we had stopped to buy our licence. The car park replaced what was a busy canal basin so it was gratifying to see that the developers had left the impressive stone portal as the park entrance.

That night we realised our two years were over: it was time to come to a decision about our future. How long ago it all seemed when we had sat in the farmhouse and talked about our exciting new home. There had been no regrets when we left our lovely house, garden, swimming pool ... looked forward eagerly as we were to a two year sabbatical before setting down perhaps a little more conservatively.

The many knocks that time had delivered over those two years served only to confirm us in a more rewarding and richer way of life. We had no regrets, despite a much harder life and a lower living standard.

But what to do now? Daft as it seems, we could now sell *Bix* for more than we paid. The money realised would enable us to buy a small cottage in the Midlands or north, and still hold on to the capital from the sale of the farm, as an investment. In any event we couldn't touch it for another six months.

'Let's stay another year' said Owen and I agreed. Or did I say it and Owen agreed, really it doesn't matter. We had proved that we could earn a living as we moved around, that we were still so happy with the life, so why not? why not?

Next morning, I lay in bed wondering whether we were behaving more like irresponsible children than a middle-aged couple. One sound resolved my doubts. Here we were, about to explore Manchester this bright October morning and as if to give us a right royal greeting, a cock crowed loud and clear. A cockerel? Yes, a cockerel. We might be only ten minutes from Manchester's Piccadilly Station, but *we* awoke to a cock crowing. And what expensive hotel in the heart of Manchester could provide that luxury?

Index